WriteTime Anthology

THREE

Short Stories by Older Writers

First Published 2024 by Shoreham Press CIC

Copyright © of WriteTime THREE – Anthology is held by
Shoreham Press CIC
Copyright © of individual works is held by the authors

ISBN Number 978-1-7385000-0-0

ALL RIGHTS RESERVED
No part of this book may be reproduced in any form, by photocopying
or by any electronic or mechanical means, including information storage
or retrieval systems, without permission in writing from the publisher.

For details on WriteTime competitions and publications write to:
WriteTime, PO Box 2206, Shoreham-by-Sea, BN43 9FU, UK

info@writetime.org   www.writetime.org

WriteTime Anthology

THREE

Short Stories by Older Writers

Printed and bound in Great Britain
By Gemini Print Ltd
Shoreham-by-Sea, West Sussex

Edited by Irene Reed and Susan Twell
Designed by Tim Gwyther
Lead Reader Nadia Mitchell
Typesetting by Marsh Graphic Design

Contents

	Foreword	1
1	The Lodger *Lynne Hackles*	3
2	A Memory of Lavender *Patricia Feinberg Stoner*	11
3	Goodbye, Benjamin *Chris Milner*	15
4	The H&M Community *Elizabeth Cathie*	21
5	Returning the Call *Carolyn Carter*	27
6	Imagine *Alun Williams*	33
7	Playtime *Brian McDonald*	35
8	Mother's Wise Words *Nicola Spain*	41
9	Farewell *Rob Molan*	47
10	Aftermath *Heather Alabaster*	53
11	The Floodgates *Moira Warr*	59
12	The House *Mark Pearce*	65
13	Turning a Blind Eye *Margaret Morey*	71
14	Just Three Words *John Maskey*	79
15	Merci *Susan Axbey*	87
16	No Further Questions *Kate Twitchin*	95
17	August 2 *Ed Walsh*	103
18	Brownie *Angela Aries*	107

19	The Census Taker *Lou Storey*	111
20	Betty's Boyfriend *Anne Thomson*	119
21	A Good Report *Graham Steed*	125
22	A Mother's Love *Sue Buckingham*	133
23	You Sent Me Flowers *David Higham*	139
24	The Reception *Ian Inglis*	143
25	A Bad Hair Day *Susan R Barclay*	149
26	Cold Hands and Bananas *Gwenda Major*	153
27	The Edge *Gillian Brown*	159
28	Ms Molly Gets Herself Noticed *Maggie Sinclair*	165
29	Perfect Rows of Little Squares *Maureen Cullen*	167
30	Trespass *Mike Watson*	175
31	Feeling Our Way Back *Marion Horton*	179
32	A Burglar's Recital *Diane Milhan*	183
33	Pterippus *Rob Nisbet*	191
34	On the Shoreline *David Miller*	197
35	Charlotte *Graham Crisp*	201
36	Clearance *Philippa Howell*	207
	Biographies	215

Foreword

Welcome to this third collection of short stories from WriteTime. Every one is the work of an older writer, drawn from the many hundreds submitted to our competitions over the past two years.

The best stories have truth at their core: the kind that makes the reader sit up and shout, however quietly.

Here you will find stories that offer surprise, hard-hitting honesty and warm connections. WriteTime aims to provide encouragement, support and recognition to older writers.

Thank you to everyone who joins in this wonderful adventure.

The Lodger
By Lynne Hackles

On January 30 the lodger, tall, white-haired and bone-jutting gaunt, ascended the stairs for the first time and disappeared into the room at the top of the house.

By mid-February the ladies were beginning to worry.

"You've never heard him, Mum? Never?" asked Susan.

Mrs Peters, marble white, lay on the bed like a knight's lady carved on a tomb lid. Through all her stillness the old lady's mind raged and her eyelids moved.

Two blinks. No.

Could it be true? Had Mr Hammond been ensconced in the attic for two whole weeks? Impossible.

"I've not seen him since he moved in but surely while I was out at work he must have come downstairs? Gone to the shops?"

Two blinks.

Perhaps he had died or left without saying. No . . . he had paid three months' rent in advance. He would not have gone away. Death then was the answer.

Death was always the answer, thought Susan. She stood, the administering angel at the coffin foot of her mother's bed. Escape could only come through death. Her own or her mother's. Two lonely women. One imprisoned in flesh. The other blood-tied to her.

The lodger was supposed to have eased their financial burden. His rent money supplemented the income from Susan's part-time job. But she had hoped for more than money. Nightly she had prayed for a friend, someone to help her cope with the useless body and eternally beating heart of her mother.

Anger rose volcanically inside her. Now she had another rotting body to contend with. She burned at the thought. Her temper, like lava, overspilled. Blistering, bubbling, it flowed through the old house. Up and up the stairs it seethed, dragging Susan to the attic.

And then, on the topmost stair, subsidence. Temper, knees, shoulders, spirit. The poor man could not help dying.

Susan crept to his door. A floorboard creaked. Her hand gripped the doorknob. The wind moaned in the rafters. A golden thread of light squeezed out of the keyhole. She put her ear against the door panel and listened. From the room came the sounds of children laughing, a chair rocking, hot coals spluttering. There were the smells of toasting muffins, brewing tea, floating chalk dust.

She held her breath. Turned the knob. Opened the door.

Mr Hammond, in the deep armchair, by the silent radio, looked up and smiled. "Welcome," he said. His eyes were bright and his sunken cheeks flushed pink. "Sit down."

Susan sat in the other armchair on the opposite side of the empty fireplace.

"I'm sorry to disturb you, Mr Hammond, but Mother and I had not seen you and we were rather worried."

The old gentleman nodded. "I told you I would be no trouble. Make no noise. That you would not know I was here."

Now Susan nodded and rose to leave. There was nothing else to say. He was not dead. He looked well. At the door she turned. "I was wondering, Mr Hammond, if . . ." She paused. "If you would mind talking to Mother sometimes. I have to work mornings and she gets lonely."

"I should be delighted, Miss Peters. Delighted."

A crackling cold waited on the landing. Frosty ferns were sketched on the skylight. Susan pulled her cardigan closer and shivered. It had been so warm in the room. So warm and yet there was no fire.

Mrs Peters had company next morning. More than she had ever expected.

Susan took coffee alone in the store's staff room, surrounded by young girls with spiky hair and long green nails gossiping about boyfriends. No-one had time for a 46-year-old spinster.

She arrived home and warmed soup for lunch. As she spoon-fed the old lady she noticed how bright her eyes were, how flushed her cheeks.

"Mum, what's happened?" And then she guessed. "Has Mr Hammond been to see you?"

One blink and an added twinkle to the eye.

Fancy Mr Hammond producing such an effect.

That evening Susan climbed to the attic but she did not see the lodger. With the ice-painted skylight above her and the threadbare carpet beneath, she sat on the top stair listening to the music, the voices, the singing and laughter. Creeping through the keyhole, seeping through the panelling, oozing beneath the door. For long hours she sat soaking up the warmth from the empty fireplace on the lodger's side of the door.

In the frozen midnight she made her way to bed and lay confused between snowy sheets.

Mr Hammond visited Mrs Peters the next day. And the next. He had time for her. Centuries of time.

Susan returned from the store each day to see new life in her mother's face. She sat on the topmost stair each night to listen at the lodger's door.

On a Wednesday in early March she had a bad headache. The store manageress sent her home mid morning. Home, unexpectedly.

Pain scratched at her eyes as she stood on the step, fumbling in her bag for the house key. Pain throbbed in time to the music, pulsated to the loud chatter. A golden thread of light squeezed out of the keyhole. Light, warmth, music, voices. She knew all would vanish at her entrance.

She stepped back and her boots crunched on the stiff white grass. The house windows burned sunshine rectangles on the chilly garden. An intruder, she peeped through the glass, through the net curtains and deeper into the room.

Eyes widened, mouth opened, knees buckled, fingers gripped the windowsill.

Her mother. Her mother, in tiers of lilac silk, was dancing with Mr Hammond. Porcelain-elegant, the figures whirled in and out between the other couples. Fairy light and agile as youth, they waltzed in the brightness. And in the ice-held garden Susan's mind screamed, *Mother can't move. She can't move.*

Shaking hands held the key, opened the door to the quiet dimness of a vast empty house. Empty save for the white statue on the bed, the lodger in the chair. Susan walked into the silence.

"I'm not well," she moaned and slid to the floor.

Mr Hammond's skeletal hands patted her face, held a brandy glass to her lips. "Miss Peters. Should I call for a doctor?"

He was all concern. With a mysterious strength he lifted her to a chair. "You work too hard. The store, your mother. You should think of yourself sometimes. Get away from it all."

Slumped in the chair she searched his eyes and found in their cavernous depths a lilac dress, a child in velvet breeches, horses, candlelight, carriages. Her pain slipped away and a tingling, glowing warmth crept in to replace it.

That night she climbed the stairs to thank him for his kindness. Outside his door she hesitated, listened for the joyous sounds, reached out to experience the warmth. There was nothing.

She knocked and entered to his command.

In the attic, years of shadows jostled with icy beams of moonlight.

"I have been waiting for you," said Mr Hammond.

He stood to join the shadows. Stars sparkled in his hair. The moon shone from the caves of his eyes. He reached out a hand to touch her and his bones glittered like ropes of diamonds beneath the cobweb skin. He tugged at her innermost thoughts. Her pain and loneliness gave him substance.

Susan blinked and looked up at the lodger, tall, white-haired and bone-jutting gaunt.

"Who are you?" Susan asked.

"Help," he replied.

"Help for me? For mother?"

He nodded.

"Where have you come from?"

"Time," he replied.

He waved a hand to illuminate the attic. Children rolled from the receding shadows. A burning log spluttered in the hearth. A nurse picked up toys and rubbed the blackboard clean.

"The Nursery," explained Mr Hammond.

He led her down the stairs and into the music-filled living room. Mrs Peters was playing the piano. A gentleman in a dove grey suit, whiskers twitching, waited to turn the music sheet. Her mother saw her and smiled.

Mr Hammond led Susan along the passage.

"A walk outside, Miss Peters?" He held open the door.

Sunshine, rose scent, bruised grass, splashing water, chirruping birds waited.

"Escape," whispered Mr Hammond.

Susan ventured forth, lifting the hem of her long turquoise gown from the pathway. Dropping the years with each step. A young man hurried across the lawn to join her.

The lodger smiled and closed the door.

A Memory of Lavender
By Patricia Feinberg Stoner

I remember.

I opened the little book of Yeats' poetry today and it crumbled out at me. The blue heads are grey dust now, but the ghost of lavender on my fingers took me back.

It was a sunny day, a rarity for Dublin. "A gift from God," he said. I smiled and said nothing. We set out for the island. *Was there an island?* I have searched for it many times since, on maps and then on the internet, but have never found it. I know we went there that day.

The ferry was an old fishing boat, the skipper grown grey and tired from battling the waves and the winds. The few tourists he could muster kept him at sea, while his sons brought home the fish. We called him our Charon, and laughed at him the way youth will always laugh at the inevitable.

As the island neared, we stepped forward, eager. We spoke of watching the sun set, but the ferryman was stern. "Last boat at six sharp. Miss it and I won't wait for you." We promised solemnly.

And the other people. *Were there other people?* There must have been, but they have melted like ghosts. I remember only him, and me. We walked along a little path, and the coarse grass pricked my feet, for I went barefoot in open summer shoes. At a stand of sea lavender, he bent and picked three stalks for me, and I rubbed their warm, furry heads between my fingers, releasing the heavy scent before tucking them into the poetry book I carried in my bag.

At the foot of a small cliff there was a cove, the path to it slippery and steep. I was afraid, but he held me firm, and at the bottom we embraced and laughed, exulting at our daring and our triumph.

Patrick. Not the Patrick I married later, some thirty years ago, but another. Padraic. Black Irish, the hair dark, dark over blue, blue eyes, the skin almost impossibly white. Padraic Aidan Duffy. Of course, everyone called him Paddy. Everyone except me. I called him Padraic, or Patrick, and sometimes Ric, and sometimes My Love.

Two days before, he had given me the little silver Claddagh ring I still keep in my jewel box. *Were my fingers ever so slender?*

The sand was soft and deep, and we kicked off our shoes and walked to the water's edge. He went in first, leapt back with a yelp and a laugh. "It's feckin' freezing!" The profanity was shocking and delicious. I didn't swear then.

We found a place, sheltered from the wind, safe above the greedy lick of the tide. We ate. *What did we eat?* Barm brack, surely, and a scrap of cheese, but not much more. We were poor, then. We drank water we had brought with us, warm now and a little stale, but it tasted sweet to us. We quoted Yeats to each other – *Will you dance, Minnaloushe, will you dance?* and laughed at ourselves for wild romantics.

We sat and watched the sun go down, and for a moment I remembered. "The ferry?" I murmured, but he shushed me and tightened his arm around my shoulder, so I snuggled into him and watched as the sky went from scarlet to palest blues and lilacs and greens, and then to dark. On the shore, far across the water, pinpricks of light sprang into life, and when we looked up, they were there in the velvet blackness above.

Later we made love under the stars. Romantic? Yes, but I remember the sharp bite of stones under my bare skin, and something – an insect? a plant? – stung me, so that I had a sore spot on my shoulder.

Afterwards he brushed the hair from my face, and looked into my eyes and whispered, "I will leave you . . . never." I stroked his cheek, and he took my hand and kissed the Claddagh ring.

The night was soft and we slept, but when we awoke the world had disappeared into white. We clung together and shivered until the sea mist lifted enough for us to make our way back up the steep rocky path. We walked towards the landing place hand in hand, and as we stood and waited for the morning ferry, he kissed me again, and again whispered, "I will leave you . . . never."

Not long after that day we parted. Why? The reasons are lost, lost with the island and the wild lavender and the tears I must have cried. Now when I call Patrick my love, when I snuggle into his comforting arm on a cold night, it is not wild Padraic that I think of. But today the Yeats and the lavender call me back, and I remember.

Goodbye, Benjamin
By Chris Milner

"Hello, Benjie, how are you doing, love? I'm afraid that Mother's here, just down the corridor looking for a coffee, but we've got a moment.

"We came right over as soon as we could, as soon as they told us you were in here, because we've been so worried, so, so worried and you're looking alright, well pretty alright considering all you've been through, just like you've had a bit of a fall, bumped your head, no-one would know, really.

"And the nurses are really kind, aren't they, and they're putting our flowers in a vase and they say it's just a question of time.

"Can you hear me in there, love? You're all so still and all that, it's hard to tell, so can you blink or something if you can hear me? No? Oh, well, not to worry, you'll be right as rain before long so just come back, won't you, Benjie dear.

"We were all so looking forward to this mini-break up at the forest weren't we, so looking forward to it, especially after all you've been through at work, and I'm sorry about bringing Mother because I know you two have your differences, don't always see eye to eye about everything, do you, and she was absolutely right about it being too wet to go walking in those little country lanes wasn't she, look what happened to you.

"Yes, I know, I know, she can be a bit rude, but that's just her way and I know how upset you were about the library and all that, but don't you worry, it'll all work out, you'll see because I expect they'll be on the up again just as soon as they get the Tories off the council, and they'll need a man with your skills and experience, someone who knows the Dewey Decimal System inside out.

"And I'm sorry about that thing with Geoffrey, you know it wasn't anything, really it wasn't, and Mother's got it all wrong, we were never 'destined' for each other, whatever she likes to think.

"No, Benjie, you're the only one for me and all that stuff at the civic reception last month was nothing really.

"Nothing."

***

"Thank you, nurse. Ten minutes? Okay. Thank you.

"Dear God, Benjie, look at you. What a mess! What a bloody mess! And all my fault. Heaven knows. Who'd have dreamed it? You ending up like this? But what could I do? I had to let one of you go. And you were always going to be the bloody one, weren't you? Show some initiative, I'd say. Presentation is everything, I'd say. Don't let the borrower walk all over you, I'd say. But did you listen? No.

"The modern librarian has to be the new renaissance man, Benjie. Were you the new renaissance man? No, Benjie, you weren't. You were obsessed with the strict application of cataloguing systems and with having the full extent of your lunch breaks. You forced my hand, Benjie. Just put yourself in my shoes for a moment.

"And then, instead of being there for Reading Week, as you should have been, I had to cut you loose and rely on volunteers to cover the shifts. Hopeless, Benjie. Hopeless.

"Anyway, I'm sorry about your accident and all that. I've left you some flowers. Hope you're feeling better soon.

"Nurse! I've finished."

***

"How's he doing?"

"Still unconscious."

"Bugger. What do the medics reckon?"

"I've asked. They're coming back."

"So, what have we got?"

"Well, he's a Benjamin Still; thirty-eight, unemployed. Contusions to his right-hand side, consistent with being struck by a moving vehicle. Blunt force trauma on his head and neck, leaving him in a coma. Discovered at the scene of yesterday morning's Tesco robbery, in the car abandoned by the gang after being rammed through the security wall.

"Wasn't found until the scene of crime unit went to work. To be honest, no-one expected to find a body in the boot. Fortunately, he was still alive but unconscious. Ambulanced here where they put him into a medical coma."

"Found him in the car boot, you say?"

"Yes, Skip."

"One of the robbers, left behind, do you think? Or . . ."

"Well, Skip . . ."

"What the hell are you two doing in here?"

"Sorry, Sister, we . . ."

"Get out, both of you. This man needs rest and quiet. He doesn't want to listen to you."

***

"Hello, Mr Still. I thought I'd just pop in and see how you were. I'll leave these flowers over here for you. Maybe the nurses can, you know, arrange them somewhere.

"You have no idea how relieved I am to see you. I just feel so bad about it all. The police only let me out an hour ago. I think they're intent on pinning everything on me, somehow. God knows how I'm going to straighten this out with the insurance people.

"But anyway, never mind me. Look at you. I nearly didn't see you at all, you know. Those little lanes are so narrow and so full of shadows, you have almost no time to react. And then, when it's wet, the surfaces are completely treacherous. I know I was going too fast. It was my uncle's funeral, and I knew I was late, so I was steaming along.

"I only just saw you in time, lying there in the ditch. You were in a right state, I can tell you. There's no signal out there, and no-one else on those roads mid week, and I'm no first-aider, and you can wait hours for an ambulance these days.

"So, all I could think of was to get you off to A&E as quick as I could. I only put you in the boot so you could lie down flat. It wasn't that easy, actually, which no-one seems to have appreciated. And very traumatic, too, which no-one seems to have appreciated, either.

"The police accused me of all sorts. Hit and run. Smash and grab. Transporting a body without due care and attention.

"And the bloody car is a right mess. You should see it.

"Anyway, I just wanted to see how you were.

"If I hadn't stopped for those fags and had the car nicked, maybe you'd have been in better shape, eh?

"And maybe I'd have been a hero."

***

"Well, Benjamin, don't you look cosy. Tucked up in your little bed. Waited on hand and foot. Toasty warm. Peaceful as the grave. Floella's gone for a break, left me to keep you company for a while. I thought we could have a little chat while she was gone. Put a few things straight.

"I'm sorry you're such a drip, Benjamin. I have no idea why Floella ended up with you. I really thought she would have made better choices. Perhaps she will now. A whole new start. I don't think you're coming back to join us, are you, dear, whatever the doctors say. It's best this way, isn't it? I know you agree. What sort of life are you going to give her, anyway? An unemployed librarian? A perpetually drunk, unemployed librarian?

"She fusses and forgives too much, my daughter. 'It's not his fault,' she bleats. Well, listen to this, dear Benjamin. You're in here because of her bloody fussing and forgiving. When you stomped off to the pub in the rain, it wasn't long before she was mewling and worrying about you, wanting me to go and find you, make sure you'd taken a hankie and had your clean underwear.

"I found you alright. Those little lanes. So dangerous, aren't they? Could happen to anyone. But, apparently, booze imbues a layer of protection and you survived.

"And now, here we are, all alone. Just you and me and this clever machinery. Oh look, I wonder what'll happen if this little line falls out?

"Goodbye, Benjamin."

The H&M Community
By Elizabeth Cathie

Something is amiss in the woodshed this cold and wintry Saturday afternoon. Something, or somebody, is in there; a thing or a body which should be somewhere else and not in the woodshed where they like to play. They've heard snuffling and shuffling.

"What is it?" the one asks.

"I don't know," replies the other, identical one.

"We should go in and look," declares one, pretending boldness.

Eight-year-old hands clasp each other as one child pulls towards the woodshed and one pulls away.

"It might be scary." Dark eyes look into the mirror of the other's face.

"It might be horrid," the mirror face replies.

"It might be a monster," the one whispers, mouth close by the ear of her twin so that the monster might not know that it is being discovered. Two hearts beating fast now. No need for words. Minds thinking alike; sticky palm clutching sticky palm. Each pushes the other towards the shed. Each pulls the other away.

"You go first."

"No, you go first."

"I said it first."

"I thought it first."

Neither child wants to open the shed door but wants the other to do so. Suddenly one leaps forward with a sudden surge of courage. She grabs the rusty door-catch with her free hand, pulls the old door open. Cries of *Nooo I'm scared* echo around her head.

The two leap backwards together. The monster tumbles out of the shed: a rolling, grunting, squishy blob of purple and green iridescent flesh.

"Arrrggh! A monster," come the identical screams, gripped hands pulling bodies close.

The monster stops in his tumbling – confused by sudden noise after the quiet of the shed. He turns his head around, leans down, looks at the two funny little human creatures, grunts sadly and then rolls himself down the garden path and over the garden gate into the field.

"A monster," one whispers.

"A monster," the other agrees.

Inside the shed the sisters see nothing amiss, everything is just as it usually is – if a little squashed by the monster.

"He was a big monster," says one.

"Huge," says the other, "very, very huge."

"Such pretty colours."

"Yes, so pretty and so shiny."

They sit on the little wooden seats. They're strangely quiet, pondering. It's getting cold with the shed door open but neither of them wants to close it. The one gives an exaggerated shiver. She tucks her hands into her pockets hunching herself into a bundle. The other swings her legs up and down, scuffing her old red boots along the dusty floor of the shed.

"The monster looked so sad," says one looking at her sister, her face blotchy red like it goes when she's trying not to cry.

"Yes," says the other, "he looked very sad." She rubbed at her nose with the back of her gloved hand. After a while she asks, in a voice incredulous with wonder, "Do you think the monster was scared of us?"

Back in the kitchen having tea and cake with their mother they're oddly quiet, not able to share their afternoon adventures with her. The one is weighing up the possibility of being allowed a second slice of cake. The other – sure that the answer to that question would be no – doesn't bother herself with such a thought. They both look towards the door when it opens to let their father come in. Through the doorway they see the dark outside and they feel the coldness of the winter afternoon around their legs as it slides in alongside him.

"I'm having a word with those community leaders again in

the morning," he says in his cross voice as he sits down at the table. "What are they called?"

"The Human and Monster Community Project Steering Group Committee," one child is very precise.

"H and M leaders," the other child less so.

"Well – whatever they're called there's a real blind spot on that corner back there. I almost ran into a monster."

***

The next morning the two return to the shed – their shed. The door is swinging gently on its hinges.

"Oh! It's empty," says one.

The other peers through the doorway with her, "Yes, empty."

"So," says her sister, "what shall we do?"

The other stands in the middle of the shed, looks around in the mode of a surveyor checking out a job, holds her chin between her thumb and forefinger and makes a decision. "We'll move out all of the rubbish then we'll put all this stuff here," she gestures towards an array of old, rusty ironmongery, "up onto the shelves. Then we'll sweep it all out and clean up the window. Then we'll bring in the blanket and the old quilt and we'll make it all nice and snug and cosy."

Her sister looks a little daunted by this list. She says quietly, "Okay."

Two hours later all is completed and they head off through the gate, into the field and then down into the wood.

"How will we find him?"

"We'll call him – but just quietly so we don't scare him."

They reach for each other's hand. Each wills the other to be brave and go first. Each is a tiny bit scared. They call, "Hellooooo! Monster! Are you there?"

"Monster, where are you?"

"We won't hurt you, Monster. We're sorry we scared you."

"Really sorry we scared you.'

And then, just as it's getting to be home time – tea and cake time – they see him; a heap of squidgy, shiny, purple and green flesh lying at the base of a big oak tree.

"Oh, Monster, there you are," says the one.

They crouch down side by side amidst the leaves and smelly vegetation.

"Don't be scared, Monster. We've made you a lovely den," says one.

"So you'll be comfy and warm," says the other.

"We'll bring you cake," they say together.

Returning the Call
By Carolyn Carter

Sister Seraphina was always close to the door, bright as a lighthouse beam ready to welcome. Perhaps she planned her escape or Reverend Mother put her there as a beacon of goodness. Her face, the most angelic in the convent, was expressive and kind, a truly happy face. In another life, Sister Seraphina might have sold holidays to jaded families. Photographed in some tropical paradise she would be a fine example of the benefits of relaxation. The caption would describe – CONTENTMENT.

I went into the convent because I win things; almost everything. I'm exceptionally lucky. Winning is expected to be a good thing. Without an element of chance, it's just familiar. Good fortune attracts attention. There were newspaper articles, television interviews and questions I couldn't answer. Sacrificing the prospect of a luxurious life had not been difficult – I needed endurance, not luck. Giving up the possibility of riches was the least I could do in return for a simple life.

Standing outside the convent, years since my unremarkable leave-taking, I realise that twelve months and two weeks inside this house of contradictions affected me more than anything in between. Silence caused frustration and made us aware talk time couldn't be squandered. We auditioned words without a sound from our lips; hoarding the most useful to surprise ourselves on dreary afternoons. For an hour after the evening meal we talked at length of the mysterious while irritations festered. Eager to speak, we measured opinions by the time it took to consider them; mindful of the bell to signal silence.

The drive is still gravel. Someone must tend it, pulling weeds to find that when they stand and stretch, the stiffness lasts for days. I hadn't planned to return - memories crowded until the past seemed more restful than the present. I thought how good it would be to walk across the gravel again and see if anything had changed.

Nostalgia stops me as I pass flower beds scented with thyme. Overwhelmed and startled, I sit on a bench and remember.

Reverend Mother called me Sister Evangeline and hoped being talkative was a blessing. Silence would be my personal challenge.

I heard they changed the laundry. No more starch or pleated bonnets. It's automated now. Sister Clare's hands no longer raw.

Nobody is expecting me. I hope Reverend Mother meant it when she said, "Come back when you're ready". Had she imagined seventeen years? Sister Seraphina won't be opening the door.

I wouldn't call it home; I'm not anticipating a welcome. Home is a place of acceptance. I've been travelling so long I've forgotten the freedoms of home. I missed the small allowance for mistakes and the comfort of settling. Most of all, as time passes I miss the pleasure of arrival. To be welcomed by someone who knows my strengths and shortcomings seems an impossible wish.

I've thought about the difficult times, the grievances stored and mouldering – Sister Mary Terese told me I shouldn't sing in chapel; my voice was irritating and nobody could concentrate. I suggested they cultivate patience.

I imagined convents were places for ideas and contemplation. The atmosphere at this one had never been tranquil, it was combative and petty. The Sisters were irritating. Arguments over soap, whether tea was too milky or starch too stiff were ludicrous but heartfelt. We were annoying and frail after weeding or laundering several hours a day; there were predictable flash points. After much effort to be tolerant and kind, we found to our surprise we were ordinary.

Silence was difficult. Not the only difficulty. A lot was caused by me, I admit. I missed my family. Reverend Mother agreed in the end I'd be useful elsewhere.

Sister Seraphina saw my disappointment. She gave me her prayer book with all her special places marked, it kept me constant. More than that, the pages were familiar and comforting, opened in silence, which I managed despite the difficulty. I travelled, found misfortune and disaster more often than seemed likely. Whether I attracted it, was drawn or sent to it I couldn't tell.

In a school on stilts above a river, a filthy surge brought disease. Many survived, more than could be expected after such a catastrophe.

Recently I tried the lottery, to see if I still had the knack. I had. I tried to make the most of each windfall, but good fortune is an illusion. Suffering continues; there's no end to it.

I wanted to even things up. A lottery win would change lives, but difficulties multiplied – there was never enough to help everyone. The responsibility of choosing between poverty and disaster was more than I could manage and my thoughts were often with the convent.

Nuns bickering over biscuits and starch seemed understandable. Even if I couldn't settle disputes, I longed for a chance to stand beside Sister Mary Terese and sing off-key.

There has been something of the goose about me. Supplying golden eggs to convents and communities has been too easy. A gift is no trouble to offer; I could do more if it were not for an inconvenient longing for the life of an ordinary Sister.

People can be wary of nuns. The truth is, like everyone else, far from being born with impossible stocks of goodness, we need time to consider what has gone before and how best to use the present. Perhaps, up to now, winning and distributing to those in need has been the focus of my life. Stopping to wonder why I have been gifted such responsibility is to challenge my existence.

I shall be a most ordinary Sister in a convent garden. Mindful of the past and hoping for understanding and kindness, I'll begin again. I am grateful for the gift of winning and the ability to change lives has been an honour. But I admit, it is all beyond me. Aware of my footsteps on the path I look through the trees to the sunlight, a shimmer of possibility.

So here I am, settling to seclusion, the comfort of routine and all the petty rituals of communal living. This time I will be patient. If silence becomes overwhelming and unreasonable, I shall remember the busyness of other days and be thankful.

I'm ready. The click of the latch is familiar. Nothing has changed. Trees leafier perhaps, courtyard bright with daisies and lavender on the wind.

The door opens. Sister Seraphina waves her arms. "Welcome home, Sister Evangeline," she says. "What kept you?"

Imagine
By Alun Williams

The birds didn't go south in the winter. Not that year or the next. They stayed.

Green fields morphed into the colour of dry sand. We thought it was great, at first. Endless sunshine and no need for foreign holidays. We flocked to the beaches and left our plastic bottles to pollute the ocean. I wrote a message saying, *Fuck You*, placed it in an empty Evian bottle and threw it into the sea off Brighton Pier and laughed as I watched it float away on the receding tide.

People laughed a lot for the first couple of years. We ignored the warnings. I mean, this was just sunshine, wasn't it?

In the third year of constant sunshine, average temperatures in the UK reached 45 degrees. The stench of smoke from charred woodland hung in the air for months and we didn't go out, except at night when it was a cooler 30 degrees. Prices rose and there were riots in the streets.

The fourth Prime Minister in as many months pointed to

the fact that we were better off than many places, we would prevail. Food became more expensive than heroin. People fought and killed for a loaf of bread and whenever rainfall came, people danced in the streets gathering as much of the scarce precious liquid in plastic containers as they could.

It's been ten years now. There are no birds anymore. There is little food. The Arctic ice has melted and the oceans have risen. Outside my home, my flood defences are failing. The ocean is part of my furniture. I live upstairs and wonder if I can climb onto my roof. I open my bedroom window and dip my hand into the rising waters. There's something in the water and I reach out to get it.

It's a plastic Evian bottle with something inside. It's a note. I unscrew the top and pull it out. It reads, *Fuck You.*

Playtime
By Brian McDonald

Four.
Teddy Edwards does tricks. Sometimes there's a puff of smoke. Not always. My model soldiers disappear then come back again. A card goes then he uses a knife to cut open an orange and it is in there. We all shout and clap him so he does a big bow then goes all floppy so that we can play with him again but Billy punches him so I hide him behind the chair so he is safe. When the other children have gone and Mummy has tucked me in, Teddy comes out again, crawls onto the bed and puts his arm around me.

Eight.
Teddy Edwards can sing some nursery rhymes and point at letters in a book and make 'ah' sounds, or 'gr' but he doesn't answer questions except to shake or nod his head. I still talk to him all the time, say hello when I wake up and after school tell him everything that has has happened during the day. If I

have got into a fight he doesn't scream or hit me, just listens to everything, always keeping his big brown eyes on mine. His head might turn if someone else speaks or there is a sudden loud noise but his attention always comes back to me. I have heard all his songs many times over but when I ask him to sing loud to drown out the shouting and banging from downstairs he always does.

Twelve.

I don't like him looking at me. Whenever I wake up and find that he's snuggled up alongside me I toss him on the floor. Eventually he stops getting onto the bed. I check the house cameras that Mum had installed after Dad left and there he is, standing outside my bedroom door, head slowly turning, scanning the landing like a tiny bouncer. I know that on the panel where the back fur has worn away, the words Guard Mode will be pulsing red.

In the morning he tiptoes in, positions himself where he can recharge and then goes to stand-by. It creeps me out. A girl that I like giggles a pitying laugh when she sees him so I start locking my door. Teddy still keeps vigil until one night, heading for the bathroom I trip over his body, swear, then kick him into the opposite wall. After that he retreats to the cupboard where we keep all the old toys.

Sixteen.
It's dark but I don't want to switch on the lights. Mum's in an alcoholic haze so is unlikely to wake up but you never know. She called the Feds on me last time. I'm looking for money preferably or, if not, something I can turn into money asap. Jewellery or watches would be good. Short of that, anything portable. With a sinking feeling I realise that everything here is junk. This is the final room and is even worse than the others, full of dusty crap that hasn't been touched in years. I open the last cupboard and jump back in shock as two shining eyes turn toward me from a moth-eaten, matted face.

"Jesus!"

I slam the door shut. I really, really need money. What the fuck am I going to do now?

Twenty.
Clearing the house is more difficult than I expected. I can't say it was ever full of happiness. But it was home and every faded photograph under a table, each notch in the woodwork, tugs at my memory. As ever the main purpose is to raise funds. I am trying to filter the contents into two groups: totally worthless, or maybe worth something. If I can find a vintage dealer then perhaps ten per cent of everything here might generate cash. Most of the toys are too damaged to be any use but teddy bears, even old models as battered as this, might hold some value. I stare into his face but there is no response. The sewn-on smile is

broken at one side and it's turned down. He looks as miserable as I feel. I chuck him into the trailer and drive away.

Twenty-four.

I am suddenly awake and scared, holding my breath until I remember that I do have to breathe. There is a plan. Get to the kitchen, through a window, then over the fence. But all that assumes prior warning. I had installed security but their software is obviously better than mine because when my eyes adjust they are already stood around my bed. A light clicks on. Four of them in ski masks. The weapons are a giveaway. Baseball bats might have meant broken bones but two machetes, a long knife, a pistol with a silencer – they say that I am dead. I start to open my mouth to plead but then think, *What's the point?*

A noise from the top of the cupboard makes them all swivel. Something flies through the air, there is a gurgling, tearing sound and I am hit by a spray of warm sticky liquid that leaves the taste of iron in my mouth.

Ducking under the covers I hear screams, shouting, the thud of the gun firing twice, then silence. I emerge to carnage. Two of my would-be killers have their throats ripped out. One has been shot and the shooter himself has Teddy Edward's arm stuck through his eye socket up to the elbow.

When I turn him over, Teddy has a scorched hole in front and a bigger one in his back. Stuffing and wires trail out into the pool of gore. Somehow the smile has righted itself and both bright pupils follow my movements. One of his paws flutters as if he's trying to reach towards me. I find myself weeping, out of relief or something else, I don't know. More men will be coming so I pull myself together, snatch my pre-packed bag and head for the door.

Looking back I see the small body lying soaked in blood. I reach down to pick up my only friend in the world and together we run out into the night.

Mother's Wise Words
By Nicola Spain

This is one of those living-in-the-past days that seeks Mary out once in a while.

The reminiscing phase usually appears unbidden, as if the gentlest of breezes has wafted it through the open window, unsettling the net curtain, and delivering those nostalgic feelings of a happier, richer and more companionable era.

An unwavering countenance in the dressing-table glass could be the reason for this morning's nostalgia. Mary has never before noticed her resemblance to her mother as strikingly as she does now, catching sight of the very thick, still-black eyebrows that suggest a disapproving librarian. They contrast starkly with her snow-white wavey hair.

Her hand traces over the engraving on the silver jewellery box. She hesitates before raising the lid, savouring the anticipation of the twirl of the ballerina with its swinging legs. On cue, the tiny doll rises from its turquoise silk bed. Sadly now devoid of its miniscule white tutu, the dancer puts Mary more in mind of a salmon leaping from the waves than a prima ballerina.

In more carefree times, her nimble fingers would swoop into the jewellery box to capture a filigree necklace or ruby ring to set off an outfit for an evening of dancing. She loved those glamorous soirees, the ladies exquisite in taffeta ballgowns and the men in tuxedos, all swirling under sparkling chandeliers.

Mary's fingers, now cumbersome with swollen joints, fish awkwardly among chains and the odd earrings. She finds the remnants of the ballet dancer's netted skirt, snagged on an open marcasite brooch. She smooths the tuille and resolves to restore the dancer's dignity one day soon. As she closes the lid, the ballerina sinks down into a tangle of chains.

She turns the ornate scrolled key in the walnut wardrobe, and creaks open the door. Her musquash coat is on the sturdy wooden hanger that has kept it in shape beautifully over the years.

Gripping the bannister tightly, she makes her way down the stairs, mindful of the third stair from the bottom where the Axminster carpet has come adrift.

Mary is almost ready to go. She gathers up shopping bags and handbag, then lifts her hat from the coat stand and places it on her head. Brown eyes peer back through the mirror.

As she opens the heavy front door, bright autumnal light floods into the oak-panelled hallway. She crunches across the pink gravelled drive and through the wrought iron gates bordering Victoria House.

She has always loved living in this road of beautiful Georgian houses with their long and well-tended front gardens. Apart from the number of cars on the drives, not much has changed here since childhood. She could never move from here – her rightful place in society. It immortalises everything she holds dear.

At the bus stop she waits, pass in hand, for the arrival of the Number 21.

Fifteen minutes later, nicely warmed through, she alights at Grainger Street and makes her way directly to the indoor market. She loves the hustle and bustle inside, the vaulted glass ceilings and stalls banked up with bananas and vast walls of apples. It takes her back to her childhood when she would accompany Mrs Roberts, who helped Mother with shopping and other household chores.

Mary makes her way to the usual stall. The greengrocer, a kindly soul, always packs her bags, taking care to ensure they are evenly weighted, so she can manage them more easily.

Her next stop is St Wilfred's Hospice Shop. Mother had always instilled in her the need to ensure that everything was put to good use, and had regularly given Mrs Roberts bags of clothing to drop off at the charity shop for those 'less fortunate'. Mary sometimes noticed that not all the things in the bag actually ended up at the charity shop and had once mentioned this to Mother.

She could remember Mother's response still. "Why do you think I ask Mrs Roberts to drop them off? It's to give her the opportunity to look through and take out anything she can use. I don't want her to think I'm giving her charity, but it's really important that we look after those who aren't as lucky as we are, Mary." She'd learned an important lesson that day.

Mary has carefully followed Mother's advice to ensure people don't go hungry or cold.

Before every Tuesday's trip into town, Mary recalls Mother's caring words, about the need to ensure those who are struggling don't go without; and those who have more than enough, have a duty to pass on their spare food. She checks her cupboard and fridge before leaving the house and always makes the food bank her last stop before taking the bus home.

As she pushes open the door of St Vincent's Church Hall, the cheerful voices of the volunteers spill out. She hesitates for a moment, then their faces split into smiles as they recognise Mary from her regular Tuesday visits. They ask how she's doing and what she's been up to this past week. Not for the first time Mary thinks how kind they are to give up their time so selflessly to help others. Mother would certainly have approved. She hands over her Marks & Spencer carrier bags to a smiling young volunteer with bright pink hair.

A short time later, Mary boards the 21 and eases her aching limbs into a seat at the front of the bus. The short journey is only just long enough for her breathing to settle. Her stop is just around the corner from home and she struggles down to the pavement with her heavy bags, desperate to reach home where nothing more is expected of her for the rest of the day.

She pushes the heavy gate open and trudges up the drive. Almost home. She puts down her shopping bags and unlocks the door. Such a relief to be home. A cup of Earl Grey is what she needs to warm her through.

Not even bothering to remove her coat and hat, she heads to the kitchen. She fills the kettle, spoons tea into the teapot and puts a cup and saucer on a tray. Minutes later she carries it through to the sitting room and sets it down on the side table next to the Ercol armchair, hoping to be warmed by the sun's rays filtering through the window. She lowers herself into the comfort of the cushions and waits for her legs to register the fact that they are no longer required to move. She'll just let her tea cool for a minute.

Mary's eyes flicker open. Her mouth is dry. She has no idea how long she's slept. The tea is now cold. She strains her eyes to see the carriage clock on the mantlepiece – 2.15pm. She's been spark out for almost two hours. Slowly she straightens her fingers and grips the wooden arms of the chair; she prises herself from the seat and straightens herself into a standing position. Her head feels too light for her body, as though it is bobbing above her on a string. Her limbs are weak. She realises she hasn't eaten breakfast before heading out this morning; she really ought to eat something, anything.

Moving slowly, she retrieves the carrier bags from the hall and carries them through to the kitchen. She has no idea what will be inside. She's always very grateful for whatever they provide. She rips open a packet of white bread buns and tears one in half and crams it in her mouth.

Thank God for the kindness of others, she thinks. Once she's eaten, she'll put on the cardigan from the charity shop. That should add another layer of warmth.

Thank goodness she always took notice of Mother's wise words.

Farewell
By Rob Molan

Aye, Sandy was right, as he often was. There were shoals of herring this time waiting out in the sea. The catch should get a good price, though no doubt the fishmonger will want to haggle as usual.

The radio crackles and the harbourmaster's voice comes through.

"Hello again, John. Can you hear me?"

"Aye, loud and clear," I reply.

"What time do you estimate you will arrive at the harbour?"

"In about half an hour."

"Okay, John, we'll be waiting."

"Fine." I'm not in the mood for conversation right now. We'll deal with matters once the boat is docked.

I grip the helm tightly, concentrating hard on steering the *Morning Mist* back through the rough sea. Dark clouds start to gather above, casting a giant shadow over the water.

The cold gets to my bones these days. That wasn't always

the case. When we were younger, Sandy and I could be out in all weathers and neither of us would complain about the wind, the rain or the icy cold winters. We were expected to get on with it – living with the elements went with the job.

I'm remembering Sandy's best man's speech at our wedding thirty years ago. He was nervous as hell at the start, but with the help of a nip or two he gained confidence and stood tall and dispensed advice to Jessie about how to put up with me; complimented the bridesmaids on their dresses, and regaled the gathering with several anecdotes at my expense. I vividly recall one of his stories:

One summer, John and I went to the horse racing at the Musselburgh course. He could never hold his drink and sometimes made a fool of himself. On one particular occasion he got as drunk as a lord and told me that he was going to the horse's mouth to get a tip for the next race. I assumed that he was going to approach someone who claimed to be in the know but blow me but didn't he go up to one of the fillies in the paddock and ask it for a suggestion!

I smile when I think of the guests roaring with laughter when they heard that tale. Sandy was a handsome lad in those days, with smooth skin and a thatch of blonde hair. The sea winds roughened his face over the years, as they have mine, and his hair greyed from the hard life we lived. Defiantly, my mane has remained jet black.

A strong wind starts to build up and the trawler is buffeted by waves. I turn it slightly downwind to outrun the gale, before eventually getting it back on course. The turbulent sea takes me back to the night when Sandy saved my life. The storm was ferocious and a gale was blowing from all four corners of heaven. I was stupid and slithered down the deck of the boat to try and prevent some baskets going overboard. He was shouting, telling me to stay put in the cabin. Idiot that I was, I went over the side and was left hanging on for dear life by one hand. He rushed over and, at great risk to himself, pulled me up with his strong arms and onto the deck.

It wasn't the first time he saved my bacon. When I was eight I climbed up a tree for a dare and found myself too frightened to get down. The other boys jeered but Sandy climbed up alongside me and helped me down slowly. That was Sandy for you – always ready to put the other person first.

I'm feeling very tired now. The day has taken it out of me; my shoulders are aching and my arms are struggling to steer the wheel. At last, I see the lights from the houses at Fisherrow harbour and I start to reduce the speed of the boat. The old girl has seen a lot in her time, providing a stage for Sandy and me to grow from boys into men as we pursued the silver darlings in all sorts of weather. It has provided the funds to pay the mortgage for the home which Jessie and I have happily lived in all our married life. But now it's paid off, I think the boat has served its purpose.

Jessie's arthritis is painful now and slowing her down, it takes her much longer to do chores around the house. If I was at home more, I could help her and she could rest up. I owe her that, after all the worry I've given her over the years, lying awake at night fearing that I wouldn't return safely from the North Sea.

As the trawler gets closer to home, I see in the fading light a police car and an ambulance, and a small group of people standing by them. Screeching seagulls fly above the boat providing a cortege as I slow it down and guide it through the mouth of the harbour. It takes the men a couple of minutes to tie up the boat in the choppy conditions. Once it is done, and I leave the cabin, I see a policeman taking off his cap and standing to attention. Then Dr Lawrie jumps down onto the boat, his white hair blowing in the wind as he strides towards me.

"Where is Sandy, John?" His steel grey eyes study me carefully.

"He is down below with the tarpaulin draped over him. He fell clutching his chest as if he was having a heart attack. God rest his soul." I bow my head.

"You get yourself onshore, John, and we'll sort things out." As I walk past, he grips my right shoulder and squeezes it.

I clamber up and steady myself and see Jessie walking slowly over, wrapped in a shawl and wearing a rain hat, a reassuring smile on her bonny face. She reaches out her arms to me and I stumble over and fall into them sobbing.

"Let it out, John," she whispers. "There's no shame in

crying." She rocks me back and forth.

After a few moments, I lift up my head and look at her.

"That's the last time I'm taking out the *Morning Mist*, Jessie. It's done us proud but its best days are now behind us." I could feel my shoulders sag as I spoke.

"Aye, I understand, John. Let's go home now. The fire is lit and I've made some soup."

The wind behind us is strong and we cling to each other as we make our way steadily down the path. Already though my mind has turned to the task which I must start on tomorrow. Sandy never found a lass to marry and have a family with, so it will fall to me to write a funeral oratory which does him proud. These words immediately come to mind:

> *"We two have paddled in the stream,*
> *from morning sun till dine;*
> *But seas between us broad have roared*
> *since days of long ago."*

— After Robert Burns

Aftermath
By Heather Alabaster

If the bird came a third time, Jack would be ready. Tucked behind the bamboos, he listened for its screech to puncture the sky. He sat alert, poised with the hosepipe across limp knees; he'd give it a proper scare today, get that racket out of his head.

So when the vivid green shape flashed across the apartment's roof garden, swerved round the canes and headed for the cordon apple trees, he was quick to spin the chair and wrench the tap to full blast. The hosepipe kinked but he gripped it tight like a rifle and caught the bird with a punch of water, sending it rocketing up. It screamed and vanished, the bamboos still quivering in their pots. Jack cheered and pumped the air, glad.

In the kitchen, Pazir dropped the potato peeler when spray hit the window. He made for the roof terrace door, his dark head jutting to peer into the clump of potted shrubs further down the garden. Jack saw him and shouted, still brandishing the hose.

"Paz, I got him! Shot the bastard. Got him side-on. It didn't kill him, but he won't be back any time soon." Jack shook the hose again, then let it drop, looking over at his companion. "He won't come back now. Will he?"

Paz chuckled. "Great shot, Jack. He's long gone, I bet you've scared him off for good."

And the large man in the apron emerged to coax the unwieldy hosepipe back onto its stand, and wheel Jack's chair towards the sunnier side of the roof. Here were two raised beds lined with herbs and a few late vegetables, backed by the trellis of apple trees. Out on the roof, detached from the jostling streets below, Jack would sit scanning the city and smoking black Turkish cigarettes.

Pazir padded back to the kitchen to get on with supper: sausage, with plenty of mash, and apple crumble – Jack's favourite. Blending fat and flour, adding sugar with a nip of cinnamon, he was thinking about the bird. It had been some five years since he'd last seen green parakeets. They lit up the dusty landscapes of Afghanistan, winging past you, swift and bold. Or else they'd hide, high in a dense canopy, guerrilla-style. If you stood a while, you might see glints of acid green and yellow, or a tail of heavenly turquoise as they ricocheted through the forest.

Pazir inhaled deeply – the scent was apples and cinnamon, but his memory led him to Kandahar in spring and the fragrant southern plains, heavy with apricot, cherry and almond blossom. Boisterous flocks of green parakeets would dart in and out of the trees feasting on the swelling buds. The air was teeming and bright with colour, as if a magician had shaken out a kaleidoscope of brilliant drops, to tumble and shimmer in the sky. In the orchards there would be farmers armed with bird scarers and nets. Pazir recalled his father setting off early down the rubbly track, melting into a pastel dawn to reach the crop before the morning ambush.

A flock could devastate a farmer's field in hours but his little sister Soraya, entranced by velvet-soft feathers and speechlike cries, had begged to keep one as a pet, wanting to make it speak her name. Instead it called out, "Pazir, Pazir, Pazir," which broke her heart, so that one day she opened the cage and shooed it away.

Pazir understood that Jack's own heart was scarred by the relentless seeking and killing of others, day after brutal day. Parakeets are not frequent scavengers, but in those hidden groves and valleys, where the dead lay uncollected, Jack's patrol would sometimes disturb a throng stripping desiccated slivers from the bones. For Jack, as they scrambled and yelled around their prize, it always seemed his own name that rang in his ears and he shrank from it, weighted with guilt.

* * *

When the cook raised the kitchen blind two mornings later, the parakeet was there, its scaly claws latched onto a scabby fallen apple, vermilion bill prodding at the softer parts. The neon-bright head swivelled at the sound and Pazir held his breath. The bird stared a moment longer, inspecting the intruder, then picked up its feet and flew off. There was no shriek; Jack still slept, peaceful and safe.

It came early most mornings after that for the apple cores and peel that appeared on the narrow service path under the kitchen window, where Jack's wheelchair couldn't go. The bird paraded round the scraps, poked, pecked and flared its beautiful tail. Pazir would watch, beguiled by soft shrouds of memory rising and wrapping round him. If it lingered, or Jack was heard stirring, he would raise his hand sharply, and it skimmed away.

One day the parakeet landed on the window ledge, fluffing and fanning wings and tail in a bobbing display, its curious orange eyes fixed all the while on the face behind the glass. Pazir instinctively rested his hand on the pane between them, as in greeting. The bird hesitated, still staring, before hurtling upwards. It seemed that now they were collaborators. Pazir found himself not delighted, but ashamed.

Throughout October, the two men prepared the roof garden for the winter season. Jack – perched on top of the beds, legs splayed – stretched out to dig cells for onion, garlic and next spring's tulips. Pazir coralled rusty leaves into crackling piles, deliberately working noisily as he went, with a watchful eye on the sky.

"Paz, I'm freezing, and it's getting dark. I say we go in – let's finish this tomorrow." Ruddy-faced and chilled, Jack lifted his arms like a child for Pazir to hoist him up, brush off the crumbly soil, and place him carefully in the chair. He wheeled himself away towards the terrace door. Then he stopped dead.

"What's that on the ground by the window? Paz – what the hell is that?"

"Looks like a feather, it's only a feather. I'll get rid of it."

"It's a green feather, can't you see?" yelled Jack, his voice thick with rage. "It's a bright green feather – it's that bastard bird again. It's back. I'll wring its neck!" He thumped both fists on the arms of the chair with such force that his slight body jolted awkwardly up and sideways and left him crooked.

"Whoa, Jack, it's alright. A bird's shed a feather flying over, or it could've blown here from anywhere. Don't worry." Pazir spread his hands in a calming gesture, but Jack's voice dropped low and urgent – almost a hiss through gritted teeth.

"Have you seen it, Paz? Has it been near us, has it been calling?"

"No, no, I haven't seen it. Not here, no."

Pazir, outlined against the setting sun, went to help his friend straighten and shifted him at his skinny waist until he was upright again.

Once inside, Jack hunched on the sofa, eyes closed but not asleep. Pazir brought rum and coke, and apple cake, which neither of them ate.

The Floodgates
By Moira Warr

It's morning. Nothing's changed. The same old question: *Why am I the only one left behind?* My image in the mirror mimics the saddest of emojis, the one with the single tear, downward mouth and drooping eyebrows. Me.

No ordinary flood this time; not the severe, sudden deluges we see on the news but an inundation that would surely outmatch the 'floodgates of the heavens' Noah encountered.

"Please someone help!" I am hoarse. "HELP!" Of course, nobody replies.

Take deep breaths and try a little acupressure, a voice says. Probably mine.

My heart continues to gallop, my right eye still twitches and the trembling everywhere just won't stop.

Three days now and no word, no sign; no evidence anyone survived. I keep hearing traffic roaring up the hill but it's only the wind. What happened to my neighbours? Where are they? Did they whizz off down the hill to plunge straight into a sea of water which is now almost lapping at my feet? Why am I still alone on the crest of the hill, waiting?

I hear all sorts of noises. The distant hum of cars, and something faint like the throbbing of a helicopter fading away. Or is it a light plane? Or . . . my old ear problem?

Right now, a lake of water surrounds the house and garden. Pieces of driftwood and debris nudge this invasive shoreline. I am thankful no grey, bloated bodies, human or animal have arisen from the depths but I smell decay in the air.

The back door rattles. Am I about to be rescued? Or murdered? Did I lock the door? NO. And now I can't move. I've been too long frozen in my sanctuary. I hear footsteps. Someone is barging in.

"Marge, are you there?" A familiar voice. Simon, my neighbour. A troubled young man.

"Simon," I almost shout. "I thought you went to town to see the doctor."

He pushes his blonde hair off his forehead and starts pacing up and down. His eyes are dark and glittery.

"Nup! Didn't want to go," he announces. "Mum said she'd pick up my tablets. Finished those off. None left. Didn't sleep a fucking wink cos. Reckon must be a tsunami, shifting of the plates or those melting ice sheets."

His hands shake as he attempts to light a cigarette butt. "No more of these left either," he says as he puffs away and moves about.

After pacing several laps of the room, he stops and glares.

"Something bad's happened. The aliens have taken over. I warned Mum and she wouldn't listen. No one listened. How about now?" He peers at me and frowns.

He's shaking. "I've seen them. They've killed off everyone except you and me."

"Simon, what exactly did you see?" I finally say.

"Look!" He points to the ceiling corner in the kitchen. "There! I fucking warned everyone!"

I see nothing, just a white ceiling corner meeting an off-white wall.

Simon rushes out, slamming the door. I slump down on a kitchen stool. My mind races. Someone needing urgent help has been left stranded with a broken-down old woman.

He raps on the kitchen window and yells, "You must have diesel. I've gotta charge my phone. I know how to start the generator."

"We used the last of the diesel during the bushfires. Anyway, I don't think mobiles work in flooded areas," I yell.

"That's not true, you haven't a clue," he snarls.

"Simon, come in and have a cup of tea." I shout. "I've boiled a pot of water on the fire. We'll hear something soon."

I don't believe one word that's rattling out of my mouth.

He marches back in and starts espousing the theories his mother Liz has mentioned to me; aliens everywhere, vaccinations only kill people, those paedophiles lurking in government and not to mention all the evil psychiatrists he's been dragged off to.

Please, Liz, come home and rescue your son.

"Stay for dinner," I interrupt after he gulps down the hot tea. Simon nods but takes off to the shed, probably to pull apart twenty years of detritus and memories to locate the elusive diesel.

It's late when he finally leaves and trudges back to his home. I did offer him a bed and tried not to show my relief when he declined.

Sleep refuses to come. Round and round go the questions. What has happened to our beautiful town nestled below us in the valley? Are there other hilltop survivors? What about relatives on the mainland?

Day six, and I'm desperate. The water is receding from the paddocks near the house but that gnawing, sinking feeling in my stomach reminds me there is nothing out there. No cars, no neighbours, no communication or electricity.

Simon's staying now and often nods off during the day. I hear him prowling about most nights, unable to sleep.

A few bottles of wine have walked from the cupboard. I'm glad he found a squashed packet of cigarettes in a jacket pocket. Chain smoking calms him.

After much scrounging, we're eating potatoes and cereal for dinner. Suddenly a noise interrupts Simon's chatter about another conspiracy. The faint throb and whine of a helicopter increases very quickly to a *chop, chop, chop* sound.

"They're after me," yells Simon. He's off.

"Come back, Simon, they're here to rescue us!" I stagger out waving a tea towel to the sky. Simon's vanished. The helicopter has disappeared too. I collapse onto the ground.

I force myself up, my creaking bones accompanying me. While my racing heart threatens to ambush me, the helicopter returns and flies low over the cow paddock, then prevaricates. Horrible moments until it finally descends, blasting the rushes and bushes nearby with a final outburst of energy.

A pair of bright beacons in yellow and red step down quickly, bending to avoid the rotor blades. A familiar figure follows.

"Liz," I screech as she rushes towards me. We sob; we hug as I feel I'm crumpling into oblivion. She suddenly untangles herself from me.

"Where's Simon?"

The angels from the helicopter have already waded into the water and plucked him from a log he's clinging to. He stops struggling when he sees Liz.

As we climb quickly into the sky I feel an overwhelming sense of sadness when I see my abandoned home and garden.

We hear many lives were saved. My family on the mainland is safe but our town of course is a mess, full of dreadful memories.

The floodgates have opened.

The House
By Mark Pearce

Last night I had the dream again. The one about the house. I don't remember seeing it before.

The house appears nothing special. It has windows, doors, chimneys. A garden with a white picket fence, daffodils and other flowers I can't name.

Inside it's a different story. I explore the house room by room. I'm looking for something but I'm not sure what, and not sure I want to find it.

I wander about aimlessly downstairs, upstairs, basement and attic. The dream is so realistic I can feel cobwebs on my face. There are goose bumps on my exposed skin. The hairs on the back of my neck stand up.

I sense the presence of another in the house. I look this way and that. But I see nothing. The feeling persists. I am unnerved by the sensation.

But, you're safe in a dream, aren't you? Nothing can actually hurt you there, can it?

I flick light switches on as I go. Though none work, the gloom lifts enough to see. I'm not sure if being able to see a bit is better.

As the light improves, I become aware of the colours. Most of my dreams are in black and white. But this one features colours, strong and vivid. Pinks, purples, yellows and greens. Not a colour scheme I'd pick.

My brain puts me on alert. There is an unpleasant odour. I hear a susurration. It's inside the house. It is the sound of many voices competing to be heard. I want to unhear it. But I can't. Try as I might to think of something else, the noise invades my mind, filling my ears. Then as suddenly as it started, it stops.

I return downstairs, to the basement. I don't know why. It is as if I was drawn by some force. Even in the basement, that same light source is enough to see by. I wander around the room. Nothing is changed. Except. A door. Not there before.

I walk to it and tentatively push. Warm to the touch, it moves inwards with a creak. Loud enough to wake the dead, I think. Then wish I hadn't had that thought.

In the middle of the room is an open coffin. Perched on a wooden framework, the centre of attention in the otherwise empty room.

The coffin isn't empty. The dream has become a nightmare.

Its occupant is a man in his fifties. About 5'9" tall and a little overweight around the waist. Greying hair kept short and tidy. His eyes are closed so I can't tell the colour. He's dressed in a smart-looking black suit, white shirt and black tie. He wears black shoes but I can't see the colour of his socks without lifting his trouser cuffs. I don't disturb the corpse.

My own eyes move again to look at his face. With a start, I say 'BLUE.' His eyes are blue. And they are open. He smiles at me. A warm, welcoming smile.

His mouth opens. I am so surprised and pleased to see no fangs protruding. He says softly in a well-educated voice, "Hello there, do you want to come in and join me?"

I turn and a hand clamped down on my shoulder. With a scream I wake.

"God, I'm so sorry, Paul. I didn't mean to scare you. It's time you were getting up. We need to be leaving in about twenty minutes."

I lie there catching my breath, letting my racing heart slow. Sally stands looking down at me. "I'm sorry," she repeats, "but we do have to get moving."

"Sorry, Sal. I was having *the* dream again."

"Oh, not again, Paul. I thought we'd got past that. We're off to Devon today, remember?"

"Of course," I reply. "Give me ten minutes."

Soon we're headed for the station and on our way to Devon. The train journey passes uneventfully. We read, play cards, doze (Sal dozes – I don't dare sleep for fear of dreaming about the house again). We chat and watch the scenery flashing by.

At Exeter Station, we get another taxi to our destination.

Cases packed in we settle back to enjoy the journey. According to the proprietor of the B&B, it is a fifty minutes drive from the station.

Despite my fears I find my eyelids drooping and I doze off. I find myself at the house again and am wandering up the front path when I hear a voice. "Paul, we're here." I open my eyes and shuffle across to the car door. Getting to my feet I wander around to the back of the car to get the luggage from the boot. Sal pays the driver and he drives away.

I turn to look. I cannot believe my eyes. We are here at *the* house. *The* house from my dream. Sal is already wheeling one of the cases up the path, bordered by daffodils and other flowers. Leading up to that door. The dream door.

"Sal, this is it. This is my dream house. More like nightmare house."

"Oh, Paul. Were you dreaming about it in the taxi? I bet that's it. It's probably stuck in your mind. Come on let's go in."

Despite my trepidation, I follow her up the path. The door is exactly like the one in the dream except this one has a name on it, *Travellers Rest*. Well, nothing too bad about that. Other than it being a bit of a cliché.

The door opens and a woman appears.

"Welcome," she says. "I'm Doris, Doris Green. My husband's in the lounge."

"STAN!" she shouts.

A man appears from a front room.

"Hello, I'm Stan," he says. "Do you want to join me?"

That does it for me. I turn and wheel my case back outside.

"Paul, Paul!" cries Sal, running after me.

"I can't stay here, Sal. That's him! The man from the dream. It's too much like the dream. Let's go somewhere else."

Looking at me as if I am being a naughty boy, she gives in.

***

"I don't know what I said to them. Words just tumbled out of my mouth. She even suggested another place round the corner."

We set off. Relieved, I don't complain about walking to the next place.

Minutes later we are in a different B&B. Not quite as nice looking as the other place, according to Sal, though infinitely better to me. We settle in and unpack our cases. Sal never mentions the other place. Nor do I.

Next day Lucy serves us breakfast. After we'd finished eating she comes over.

"Well, what a lucky escape you had."

"What do you mean?" asks Sal.

"*Traveller's Rest*. It burned down last night."

Turning a Blind Eye
By Margaret Morey

"Psychopath." She kind of mutters it under her breath, but I think she wants me to hear. I pretend I haven't, because I don't know how to react. I say nothing, that way I won't cause an argument. His family don't do arguments. They'll go to any lengths to avoid confrontation. But his brother's dear wife, not sharing this gene, cannot resist stirring the cauldron, surreptitiously. When it's just the two of us, and no-one else is in earshot, that's her moment to strike.

My son, her nephew, runs ahead of us on the mountain path. He's brandishing a stick, his makeshift sword, slaying saracens. He tries to engage his cousin by waving the stick near his head. She mutters again, "Always got to be killing something . . . murderer in the making."

I half-want to say, *Can a six-year-old be a psychopath?* Or, *It's just pretend. He's a very caring child. Rescues spiders out of the bath and takes them out into the garden.*

But I've trained myself in the art of not rising to her bait.

So I say nothing.

Her son, my nephew, ignores the brandishing of the sword. Being two years older, he has tired of sticks and trots along beside us, carrying the mobile phone he got for his recent birthday. He's measuring the walk.

"I've got an app that tells us how far we've come." He looks in my direction to see if I'm impressed with how important he is, now he has his own phone. Then he turns his attention back to his mother.

"We've done three miles now . . . how much further is it . . . when are we having our picnic?"

The brothers stride out in front, deep in conversation. This is the way it is on these family days out, which means I always get landed with her.

"Ah, here we are. The top at last."

"Smashing view! You can see the sea in the distance."

"We've been lucky with the weather . . . you can see for miles."

"There's a bank of cloud out towards the sea . . . should be down before it reaches us."

"Bags I sit here."

"Who wants a sandwich?"

"Smile, everyone. Say cheese."

Click. The perfect family.

The way down is a scramble. My son is slaying monsters now, with a different stick. This one is bigger, more menacing.

"Watch what you're doing," I say, guiding him along where the path drops away steeply on one side.

Is this the best place to bring two small boys? I ask myself. But the men have planned it, and we're committed.

" . . . poke somebody's eyes out," I hear her mumble.

"Careful . . . " I reinforce her concerns, ignore the hostility.

She and my nephew are ahead of us. I can hear his high-pitched chatter, "Getting on my nerves . . . always wanting to be a knight . . . he doesn't have a phone . . . 'cos he's not eight like me . . ."

I strain to hear her answer. " . . . blinking psychopath . . . being eight won't make any difference . . . doubt he'll grow out of it. "

We catch up in time for me to see her sniff and tweak his scarf, pat his shoulder, a sort of seal of approval on her perfect child. *Does an eight-year-old understand what a psychopath is*, I wonder. *And is it a good idea to tell your child that his cousin is a potential murderer?*

The sun goes, like someone has switched the light off. A bank of cloud has massed ahead of us. A change in the weather is forecast, but we should be down before then.

"For goodness sake, throw that stick away. You're holding us all up."

My son ignores his aunt and makes some more swashbuckling noises. I feel a perverse satisfaction that he's taken no notice of her. My nephew clicks his tongue in annoyance, like a miniature adult. The two of them have got between the two of us on the path. Wisps of mist have come out of nowhere and are swirling in front of us. I want to be next to my son, to help him down, but I'm side-lined, left to bring up the rear. The murmur of the men's voices rumbles down below.

"Come on, chop-chop."

She hustles my son along the path, increasingly irritated by his stick fantasies. The mist is getting thicker and wetter, it feels as though it's raining. She stops to put up her hood and pull the waterproof cover over her rucksack. In that brief time my nephew has scrambled past her.

The two boys are ahead and I can't see them, partly because of the mist and partly because the path is full of twists and turns. I'm worried that there could be a cliff-edge ahead. This isn't family-friendly any more. I should never have agreed to it. I dare not squeeze past her. I can imagine a sheer drop below me. I try to delete the idea from my mind. *Click*. But it's still there.

I can't hang behind any longer.

"Can I get past?"

She presses herself into the hillside. It's like overtaking on a hairpin bend. The visibility is getting worse. Through the mist I can make out a shape. I think it's my nephew. It's definitely his voice.

"Hurry up."

In the absence of his mother, he's the adult, his cousin the naughty child who needs to be kept in order.

Then, through the gloom comes a rattling of stones, followed by a long silence, before a wail goes up. That's my son. Has he fallen? Is he hurt? Does he have a grazed knee or is he about to tumble to his death?

"He tripped."

My nephew is straight out with it. He's not looking at me. He's studiously killing aliens on his phone. My son is on his knees at the edge of the path, clinging on to a bush which has broken his fall. His small body shakes with big sobs. He's overcome by the shock of it all.

"You should have been watching where you were going, instead of playing with that stick," says my always-right sister-in-law.

I sit on a boulder, lift him onto my lap, and roll up his trouser legs to examine his knees. One is red and grazed, but it will be alright until we get down. The sobs are getting less. He lifts a face, wet and red with tears, from my chest.

"He pushed me."

I smooth his hair and fasten his jacket.

"Pushed you?"

"Yes, he said he was going to call for help . . . on his phone . . . said they might come and find my dead body."

"I did not," says my nephew. "That's a lie."

He's still focussed on his phone.

"That was very sensible to think of getting help," says his

mother. "But sometimes people don't understand when you try to help them."

It's hard to tell through the thick mist how far the hillside drops away, but it makes me shiver. I take my son's hand.

"Never mind. We'll go down together. Hold on to me."

My nephew and sister-in-law are behind us. No-one speaks.

At the bottom, we come out of the mist. The men are waiting by the cars.

"Ah, here they come."

"Well done."

"Who wants a drink and a biscuit?"

"Quite a change in the weather now."

My son stands beside his father, looking up.

"He pushed me over."

"We're all down safely. That's the main thing."

"I could have used my phone to get help."

"I'll get a plaster for your knee. Good job that bush stopped you falling over the edge."

"Could I have died if I'd fallen down the mountain?"

I don't want to trivialise the incident. Neither do I want to frighten him.

" . . . hard to see how far it was . . . probably not . . . might have broken a leg or something . . . "

"Time to head home."

"It's been a great day."

"Must meet up again soon."

"Perhaps a valley walk next time."

Their car pulls away. It's a silver evening, with the sun glimmering between the clouds.

"Going to be nice for the drive home," says my husband.

We follow their car out of the car park. Brother-in-law is waving, sister-in-law is looking for something in her handbag, nephew is on the back seat, probably still killing aliens.

Just Three Words
By John Maskey

The jangle of the bell gave me a welcome break from sorting out boxes of junk that no one wanted.

I looked up to see a man struggling to manoeuvre a large suitcase through the door. He was in his sixties, well dressed and grinning broadly. His smile provided the only brightness on that grey, misty morning when rainclouds had done their best to snuff out the mid-morning light. He managed to get the case through after taking some of the peeling paint off the door frames.

"Good morning," he said, still smiling. "I would like to donate these."

He heaved the suitcase on the counter and opened it. There were scores of CDs and cassettes.

I groaned inwardly but smiled my thanks. When people make a donation they feel good about themselves. They're helping a worthy cause. And it's important we go along with that. The cassettes would go in the bin, no one wanted them these days. Some of the CDs looked fine but there would be little demand for the more obscure performers.

The man fished another disc out of his pocket and held it out for me to take.

"I want you to have this. You personally." His smile dropped and he took on a serious demeanour.

The scratched plastic box did not have an album cover and the disc had no name of the band or singer. Someone had written *Just Three Words* on it with a black marker pen.

"What is it?" I asked, feigning interest.

The man's eyes lit up. His broad smile returned.

"Listen to it. It will change your life."

Yeah, right. I thanked him for his donation and he wheeled his empty case away with a cheery wave.

I spent the next few minutes sorting out the CDs, binning the ones that wouldn't sell and categorising the ones that might, just might, bring in a pound. I put them on the shelf along with the one the strange man thrust into my hand,

He returned the following morning lugging the suitcase. He grinned and opened the case on the floor. It was too heavy to lift on to the counter. It was filled with books. Most were in great condition. This was more like it.

As I lifted some of them on to the counter he studied the racks of CDs.

"Have you listened to this yet?"

He held aloft the one which said *Just Three Words*.

I shook my head. "I haven't had time."

His smile never faltered.

"Then make time. I promise you, your life will change beyond all recognition when you listen to this. It won't take long, believe me."

He was either a religious zealot or a New Age loon.

"I bought a used car a few weeks ago and when I tried to play some music I found this in the CD player. So I listened to it. Guess what was on it?"

I shrugged my shoulders, wishing he would get to the point and clear off.

"There, look at what it says."

He pushed the CD towards me.

"Just three words."

"Exactly, that's all I heard, just three words and my life has changed dramatically."

"What were the three words?"

"It said: 'give everything away' and that's what I'm doing."

Yep, New Age loon.

"I've spent my life in the pursuit of money. I collected things, I hoarded things. I thought possessions would bring me happiness, that they were a measure of my success, or would enhance my status. How foolish I was. But now I'm giving them all away and I feel liberated. I had thought the possessions would bring me fulfilment but they haven't, they've weighed me down."

"Well, that's very interesting but I'm rather . . . "

"I was so grateful that I went to the man whose car I bought. I wanted to thank him for what he did. And guess what?"

He didn't bother waiting for a reply.

"There were three different words for him. He found it on the table of a pub. He'd asked the landlord if it was his, but it wasn't. It was just lying there. So he took it home and played it. His three words were 'give up alcohol' so he did. And his life is so much better now."

Was this bloke on drugs?

"Please listen to it. Your life will be enriched. And then give it to someone else. Who knows how many lives have been transformed by this. By passing it on, we can change the world for the better."

Then he was off, trailing his empty suitcase.

I smiled as I watched him leave the shop. He may be off his rocker but he seemed harmless enough. At least he provided some light relief.

There was no need for me to give up alcohol as I wasn't much of a drinker. And as for giving everything away, well, a series of failed marriages had seen most of my possessions disappear, and I had learned to live without them.

Volunteering at a charity shop is just what I needed after losing my job and my third wife. Being in lockdown just after a divorce was bad enough, then the company I worked for soon went to the wall. There was a lot of time to fill – and I was the only one who could fill it.

I didn't hold out much hope of other work at my age and being at home watching TV all day would have driven me mad. So when shops were allowed to open as the pandemic restrictions were lifted, I volunteered to help out. Thankfully, the charity needed me as much as I needed them.

The next hour was spent going through the strange man's latest donations. His books were excellent, with some unusual ones in folio edition, pristine and unread.

These wouldn't go on the shelves. The people around here were only interested in cheap paperbacks. We would contact a book dealer about the good stuff and he would give us a decent price for them.

As I was sorting them a woman came in to browse the jigsaws. She had the look of many middle-aged women around here, tired and beaten. It was if life had dealt her too many blows. She selected a puzzle and took it to the counter, a pound coin in her hand. She picked up the *Just Three Words* CD lying on the counter.

"What's this?"

Without going into too much detail I told her about the man who brought it in and how he said it changed his life. I had trouble keeping the amusement out of my voice.

"So it's one of those self-help things, is it?" she asked.

I shrugged. "Dunno, I haven't played it."

"How much is it?"

I smiled. "Make me an offer."

She didn't return the smile but rummaged among the coins in her purse and pulled out a 20p piece.

"Will this do?"

I nodded and rang up the sales and bid her farewell. She didn't reply.

The following morning the woman returned to the shop seconds after I had turned the CLOSED sign to OPEN. She looked different, younger, vibrant even. In her hand was the CD she had bought yesterday.

"I want to bring this back and apologise to you."

She opened her purse and took out two £20 notes.

"I want to give you this. I'm sorry but it's all I can afford at the moment. I paid you a measly 20p for that CD, but what it has done for me is priceless."

My jaw fell open. "What happened?"

"It was exactly three words, just as you described it. A voice said, 'call your daughter'." Tears formed in her eyes. "We fell out years ago and she moved away and we hadn't spoken since. I missed her but was too proud, no, too stubborn to make the first move. And Jane, my daughter, felt exactly the same."

She was smiling as the tears fell freely and made no attempt to wipe them away.

"She's married now and I've got a granddaughter I haven't met. But I'm travelling down to see them at the weekend. I can't wait. I've never felt this happy in a long, long time. And I owe it all to you and that CD."

She slapped down the £20 notes and left the shop.

I picked up the disc. Trade was slow at this time of day so I put it on while I filled the kettle. I cranked up the volume.

All I could hear was the sound of an electronic hiss from the speakers. As I looked for some digestive biscuits in a cupboard the CD player burst into life.

A male voice said just three words. There was no mistaking what was said because the speakers were at full volume.

"Find true love."

Then seconds later, you walked through the door.

Merci

By Susan Axbey

It's a hot day and we're sitting under a tree on The Green eating our sandwiches as usual. It's 1915 and the war in Europe is into its second year.

"I'm not volunteering," I tell Philip for the hundredth time.

"Neither am I, Henry."

A lot of boys our age have already left England to fight, but not us. We're the bright boys, the lucky ones who stayed at school a bit longer than the others and now we've got jobs in the civil service. We run between government offices carrying messages or putting files of papers in the right order. They call us office boys but we like to tell people we're on Official Business and that we're part of the War Effort. Of course, we're proud of our brothers and old school-mates who've gone to fight. All brave lads, everyone agrees.

We finish our sandwiches and I carefully fold up the greaseproof paper which my mother will use again for tomorrow's lunch. We sit back and look around The Green.

There are some fine houses and well-off families here.

"Look. Look, there she is."

A woman has come to the gate of her house and waves us over. By the time we reach her, we are no longer Henry and Philip, the English office boys. With the help of the French we learned at school, we have become Henri and Philippe, the Belgian refugees. We greet her with shy smiles. We pretend to be sad.

"Bonjour, Madame."

"Bonjour, boys. How are you today?"

"Très bien, Madame."

"I have some cakes for you. Gateaux."

"Oui. Gateaux. Très bien."

"Help yourself. Go on, take some for later."

"Merci, Madame. Merci beaucoup."

We take two or three cakes each and walk away quickly. When we get to the other side of The Green, we collapse on the ground, laughing.

"Merci, Madame."

"Très bien."

"Gateaux."

"Merci. Thank you, Madame."

"Shut up! She'll hear us."

"Merci beaucoup."

It's a great joke. We lie on the grass, eat the cakes, and feel pleased with ourselves.

The real Belgian refugees continue to arrive. Some of them set up small shops. There is a baker and a shoe-mender.

The war goes on. We've stopped playing tricks on people now. In 1916, conscription is introduced so Philip and I will be called up when we're eighteen, which will be soon. I wonder if he is frightened. We still like to joke a bit.

"Parlez-vous français?"

"Oui, monsieur."

"But it won't bloody help you."

"There might be French girls. Or Belgian girls."

"In the trenches? Don't be an idiot."

"Well, good luck anyway."

"Merci. Merci beaucoup."

It won't be long now. Philip goes first and soon after I'm called up too. I don't know where it'll be. I'll survive, I just know I'll be all right. But on the journey out I suddenly feel so frightened I think of jumping off the train and running away. Then one of the lads cracks a joke and another starts up a song.

Now I'm here in the trenches in France and I tell myself to just concentrate on staying alive which sounds stupid, I know. Of course, gunfire might kill you but there are other things I had never imagined.

The mud is slimy, thick, and deep. Once I got sucked down and it took three men to get me out. I spit out flies every day. At night there are rats. They gnaw through your haversack. I hardly sleep it's so cold. We lie down close to each other, for warmth. But we stink. We have lice.

There are three lines of soldiers on the battlefield. I'm a runner taking messages backwards and forwards. Just like an office boy, all part of the War Effort, ha ha! I wonder where Philip is now.

Sometimes it takes me two hours to go eight hundred yards. Shells explode and I can hear the cries of men who have been hit. I try not to see the dead and wounded. Some men pray out loud, others silently with their eyes closed. I just keep saying to myself, *I'll be all right, I'll be all right*, over and over. It works somehow because finally the war ends and I'm back home, alive and in one piece.

I'll try to forget the war but before I can get on with my life I have to see Philip, who was wounded. I don't know exactly what happened to him. I'll take him something, but what? I walk through town past the row of Belgian shops. They're still here – the refugees. I go in the baker's and buy a bag of small cakes, some with raisins, some with chocolate.

Philip is in a Home with other wounded soldiers. It's rather a grand building, almost royal. He's lucky to be here, I think. Perhaps he'll get out soon. We can have a drink in the pub on the Green. In the vast lobby, men sit together on a row of seats or in wheelchairs. Some have lost a leg, or both legs. Or maybe an arm. Thank God that's not me. I try to smile at them. I pretend to be cheerful.

"All right, boys."

But their faces are mostly blank. I ask at the reception desk and I'm told Philip is on the first floor. I go up the stairs. There's a long corridor and I can see rooms on either side, each with six or eight men lying in bed. I try not to look. A nurse comes towards me.

"Oh, Philip. He's just along here. I'll show you."

"Thank you. How is he?"

"He's got his own room. Here we are."

I follow the nurse into the room. There's an empty bed and someone sitting in an armchair. The nurse is bending over so I can only see his feet in the slippers, and his knees under the dressing gown. At least he hasn't lost a leg, I think. That's good. Then the nurse moves away and it's so horrible I have to grab a chair and sit down. The face is mangled, collapsed somehow. It's hardly human.

"That's not him."

The nurse takes another chair and sits next to me.

"It is. It's Philip. Shrapnel. I'm afraid there are a lot like him here. It's not just arms and legs, you know."

I force myself to look. The face moves.

"Can he see me?"

"Yes. And we think his hearing is okay. I'll leave you together for a bit. Talk to him. It'll help."

The nurse leaves the room and I sit here, holding the bag of cakes, unable to speak. I look at the face and then have to look away. I look back. The face moves again. I have to keep reminding myself that this is Philip. Eventually, somehow, I start talking. I gabble. I know I'm saying all the wrong things.

"Yes. It's me and well, yes, it's really you, Philip. After all. You probably don't even recognise me. Maybe it's not a long time, but a lot's happened. This bloody war. Well, it's over now. How are you feeling? You must have had a terrible time. Wasn't much fun, was it? There are men downstairs who've lost their legs. I hope they're looking after you all right here."

The nurse has come back. I'm so relieved. I don't think I can go on much longer. She sits down next to me and pats my hand. Am I – Henry – the patient now? The nurse sees the bag of cakes I've brought.

"What's this then?"

"Oh, cakes. For Philip."

"He'll probably have one now, won't you Philip?"

I think the nurse is just being kind, pretending that Philip is able to eat cakes. Anyway, I put the paper bag on his lap. I don't know what to do. I take a cake out of the bag and put it in his hand. The face moves and Philip – I have now accepted that's who he is – Philip speaks.

"Gateaux."

"Oui, Philippe. Cakes."

"Très bien, Henri."

"It's good to see you, Phil."

"Merci, Henri. Merci beaucoup."

The nurse is delighted and amazed.

"Well. Those are the first words he has spoken since he's been here and they're not even English."

I suddenly feel sick. I want to leave and so I stand up. I look at the nurse.

"Sorry."

"You know you can visit Philip at any time. It will do him so much good."

On my way out of the Home, a man with no legs in a wheelchair smiles and calls out to me, "See you next time, mate." But I never go back.

No Further Questions
By Kate Twitchin

I leaned against the kitchen sink, watching his blood creep slowly across the tiled floor towards the fridge. I was panting and sweating from the effort of the last few minutes.

Waiting for my heart rate to come down, I stood there for what seemed ages in a dreamlike state. I wasn't aware of what I was thinking but my subconscious was busy getting things straight.

When I came to, I felt incredibly calm and relaxed. I liked that feeling and didn't want it to end.

This is what they don't understand. One of the things. They think I should have been desperate to get everything sorted out. Dispose of the body, clean the kitchen, establish an alibi, get my story straight.

* * *

"You made no attempt to conceal the body."

This one, a new one, asks. Are you asking me, or telling me? You've got the file, it's all in there.

"I couldn't be bothered," I tell her, same as I've told all the others.

There was no way I could have carried him out to the car. I knew that any practical method of disposing of the body would have been difficult and messy, and exhausting.

Just cleaning up the pool of blood on the floor and the spatters on the cupboard doors made me think of the worst kind of dreary housework. We'd always shared the household chores, taking it in turns to vacuum and dust, clean the bathrooms and put out the rubbish. He was hopeless at ironing and I was useless around lawn mowers, drains and gutters, so those jobs were mine and his respectively. We were a good team, we complemented each other.

"Can I go back to my cell now, please?" I ask her. Sophie. Sophie Something.

"Just a little longer, if you could, I'd be grateful, I . . ."

Dear little thing, nervous as a kitten. What on earth made her choose psychology, criminal psychology, as a career?

* * *

"Had there been any violence in the relationship before that night?"

No, I told her, never. Our marriage was good, we were happy together. Buying furniture, hanging wallpaper, learning to cook, how to wire a plug; it was all good fun. We became adventurous over the years and did some ambitious DIY, working well together. We laughed when we bricked up the external door to a coal-house and knocked down the wall inside to make the kitchen bigger, joking about how easy it would have been to brick up a dead body in that little room. Ha ha.

* * *

"You didn't have children, why was that?"

None of her bloody business. None of their business, and why they keep on asking defeats me. I've often wondered if my human rights are being violated or something but I've never bothered to pursue it. My answer is always the same: we didn't want children, we didn't need them. We did everything together. We liked to cook; chatting as we chopped onions and stirred sauces. When he went on a twelve-month secondment, working away from home all week and separating us for the first time in our married life, I would search the recipe books for something new and delicious for the homecoming meal. I was preparing to cook on that Friday night, fillet steak and mushrooms, nothing fancy because it was the dessert that had the wow factor. I'd put the cast-iron griddle pan on the hob, ready to be heated to a searing temperature when he got home.

* * *

"Tell me how you first met."

Dear little thing. I don't mind this one. I mean, I'd rather be back in my cell but it's nice to take a trip down memory lane.

Well, we were in the Sixth Form Common Room with its purple paint and abstract art, hessian on the walls and Led

Zeppelin climbing their Stairway to Heaven. I looked up from my book to find him standing in front of me.

"Ben," he said, and smiled.

I smiled back and thought, *There you are*. I had the most profound feeling that I'd found something I didn't even know I was looking for.

"There you are," I said aloud.

"Here I am," he said, still smiling.

He was nearly eighteen I was only just seventeen. We were married three weeks after my twentieth birthday.

We bought our first house, a dark Victorian terrace, no heating, no washing machine and a condemned gas oven. We stripped the old woodchip wallpaper from the chimney breast and I wrote *I love Ben* in huge letters on the bare plaster. It was only a standard HB pencil but, boy, did it take some covering. At least four coats of Dulux, which we could ill afford; we didn't have much in those early days. Isn't that a lovely story?

* * *

"What problem did killing this person, this, er, husband, your husband, er, solve for you?"

If I wasn't a convicted murderer I'd go over and give her a hug. She's trying so hard. I think she's doing some sort of post-grad paper; working on stuff for her CV. Look at her, with her smart clipboard and scratchy pen, and big compassionate eyes.

I've been studying, too. I took some books out of their library, from the rarely-visited shelf labelled *Psychology & Self-*

help. I thought I'd do a bit of self-analysis, just to show willing, to humour them. It was quite interesting, actually. I read a load of books, did some questionnaires, and was able to confirm what I'd known all along: I acted in self-defence that Friday night.

When I heard his key in the lock I went to light the gas under the griddle pan. As he came into the kitchen, the look on his face stopped me in my tracks.

"Are you okay?"

"I've fallen in love with someone else," he blurted out, "I've fallen in love with someone else."

The cast-iron pan caught his shoulder and he toppled forward onto his knees. As I brought my arms back, both hands around the handle because the pan was very heavy, he turned his head to look up at me. The second blow hit his temple and he slumped down to lie on his side. He was motionless when my third swipe smashed into his nose and cheekbone, and that's when the blood started to flow. I don't know how many times I struck him. I didn't count. I didn't expect to be asked.

They say that people who commit crimes of passion don't know what they're doing, they see red, literally see red. I saw red, the red of his blood, but I also saw the pan rising and falling, swooping through the air and crashing into his skull over and over and over. I saw everything very clearly.

Sophie Something watches me, no doubt waiting for a profound response, but I've forgotten the question.

She senses that she's losing me, she's not going to get many more answers today.

"Do you think you're evil?" she asks.

She'll have read the newspaper articles with their lurid headlines about my arrest and trial. She'll know that my barrister pleaded temporary insanity. He argued that I'd loved Ben devotedly since I was seventeen. He asked the jury to consider how Ben's betrayal after thirty years of happy marriage had impacted my mental state. He said I wasn't evil. And he was right, is right.

"No, I'm not evil."

"Do you regret what you did?"

She scribbles something on her clipboard and looks up, a little frown on her fresh face. She's going to hear some horrible things during her career and my heart goes out to her. But I've had enough for today. I don't like all this introspection; I just want to be left alone to read until it's time to go home. I'm enjoying having time to read. I can do good behaviour.

Regret? I wish I could tell her that I regret what I did. They like that sort of thing in here. The thing is, I knew in the split second after he'd spoken that the hurt was only just beginning. There would be more to come, much more. I knew that in the days, weeks, months and years ahead I would be mentally assaulted, emotionally punched and kicked, over and over again. Selling the house and dividing up our possessions; finding myself somewhere to live; hearing that he had married her; bumping into him and his new love in the supermarket; hearing her laugh at something he said; seeing her pregnant with his child possibly. So many opportunities for him to wound me.

I knew that I would suffer; he would strike me over and over and over for the rest of my life. So, no, I don't regret it, because he started it, he struck the first blow. I acted in self-defence.

August 2
By Ed Walsh

Teresa and I meet up every year on August 2. We meet in the town where we used to live together, where I still live, the town where our daughter died. She was six when it happened, and it was leukaemia that took her. It was all pretty quick, which is the best that can be said. While it was happening, we were practically living at the hospital, but from start to finish it was only about four months. August 2 is the anniversary.

We had been together for nine years when it happened, and now we have lived apart for ten. It wounded us so badly that we could barely look at each other, and after a year or so of sullen silence we decided to go our separate ways. We agreed that one of us had to stay close to where we buried her — we couldn't leave her out there alone. Because I worked in the town, that was me. It wasn't our home town, but I had been there a long time. We live nearly three hundred miles apart now.

We had met at a conference, where on the first morning we happened to be seated next to each other. Immediately I saw her, I knew there would be something between us. I had had relationships before, but as soon as I saw her, I got the strong feeling that they had only been stepping-stones towards her. And later she told me that it was the same for her, that it seemed like I was the one she had been waiting for. I was glad to hear that, because nobody had said anything like that to me before.

I was twenty-nine at the time, she was twenty-seven. Just by coincidence, we lived in towns only twelve miles apart. Even if it had been further, we would still have been together.

For the first two years, during which time we became married, we had not given much thought to having children. We had a good life with well-paid jobs, we travelled a lot, and wanted for nothing. Then our child came along and we didn't go away so much, and we didn't miss it. Teresa gave up her job to stay at home with her. She had worked at some investment firm and was highly regarded – they said there would be a place back there for her whenever she felt like it, but she never went back.

I don't know what she does now, or if she does anything. We don't really talk about those things, although she sometimes lets things slip.

For instance, I know she has three kids – two girls, one boy, or maybe the other way round. I don't know their names. She might have guessed from the fact that none have been mentioned or alluded to that I have not had other children.

I know that the father of her children is called Terence; she mentioned his name once and I could tell that she wished that she hadn't; we both wished that she hadn't but it just slipped out.

A priest came in, paid by the hospital I suppose. I took against him on principle, resented his piety, his sanctimonious platitudes, the handshake for me, the hug for Teresa. I wanted to ask him why his god would allow a six-year-old, who had done him no harm, to get so hopelessly sick. But Teresa, who had shown no previous interest in religion, seemed to be comforted by his optimism and his talk of hope and reunions beyond this life. She seemed happy to see him every time he came uninvited into the room. But maybe he was just someone other than me; me, who could find no words of hope or comfort and had nothing to say about reunions.

So, we meet once a year. To each other, we say you're looking good, and one of us is not lying when we say that. Age suits some women and Teresa is one of them, better for the small accumulations of flesh and the lines around her eyes.

We meet at the gates and hug and we buy our flowers. Then we walk up the rows and lay them on her soil gently, as if not to make any disturbance, as if wishing to keep our daughter's death a secret from her. And Teresa spends a long while on her knees, minutely rearranging the stems, as if making adjustments to a child's clothing. And then we stand a while in silence, not sure of who should make the first move away from the grave, be the first to break the spell. It is always me.

Then we go to The Boylan, a hotel a few miles out of the town, always the same place. It was where we went after the funeral, just the two of us, famished after barely eating a meal for months. That time, we booked a room and stayed a week, unable to face our home and the swing in the garden.

And now when we go, we have lunch. I drink a beer and we drink a small amount of wine. We don't have a lot in the way of conversation; some references to people that we knew, the disasters in their lives, the disasters in the world. Yesterday, we talked about the Bataclan attack, which had happened the week before. I imagined our daughter, who would now be the same age as many of those kids. At least she won't face such horror.

Later we hug again, and leave in the late afternoon, back to our second lives. They might recognise us at the hotel now, and if they do they must think it odd, the same people on the same day every year.

Liza, her name was Liza.

Brownie
By Angela Aries

Brownie, that's what we kids called her. It was nothing to do with the little people, the fairies in the glen, you understand, or the wannabe girl guides, who nowadays seem to opt for the scouts. No, it was simply because she always wore brown, from head to toe – brown hat, brown mackintosh, brown shoes.

It was the hat you noticed first of all. It was of misshapen felt, as if it had been kicked around in the dust like a football. She wore it with the brim pulled down hard over her ears, hiding whatever hair she might have had lurking underneath. Right in the centre of the crown was a symmetrical hole, roughly the size of an old penny piece. Had she cut the hole herself to let the air in (or out), or was it the result of constant tugging at the brim? We never stopped to wonder.

She was a sad figure really, shuffling along the pavement in her boat-shaped lace-ups. They were scuffed and worn down at the heels, exposing the rough hard skin of her ankles. One sole flapped loose, and was most likely the reason for her strange gait. Like her footwear, her legs looked tired and run-down – little pink sticks, swollen scaly blue and red with chilblains at the base.

We children recognised the signs, being only too familiar with Granny's patent cure. This involved pouring boiling water over mustard powder in a chipped enamel bowl, and immersing your poor injured feet for as long, and as often, as you could bear it.

However bitter the weather, though, Brownie never wore socks or stockings. Maybe she didn't have any. Come rain or shine, winter or summer, she always looked exactly the same.

We were curious at first, and used to dare one another to get up close, without her noticing. We soon stopped that though. One look from those vacant brown eyes, set deep as a pit in her ravaged face, was quite sufficient. Besides, she smelt, and badly. If ever we chanced to meet her in the street, we'd step into the road smartly, and scuttle past.

Brownie became an object of fun. We often used to spot her shambling along the main road as we were getting off the school bus. "Brownie, Brownie," we mocked and taunted. But however much we cat-called there was never any reaction.

One day they dared me to sneak up behind and pinch her. There was a pained whimper of surprise and shock, then the cowed figure shrivelled up even further, and hobbled away. I felt no shame.

From being an object of curiosity, Brownie became a source

of suspicion and fear. It was whispered she was a witch, she brewed evil potions, she could even put a curse on you. Odd unusual incidents were quoted as examples; the collection of lean cats that tailed her down the alley, a horse that had run amok, the dog that had died. Her eyes became inflamed, her nose elongated, and covered with spots, her teeth blackened. The brown mackintosh became a sinister black cloak.

We invented stories and started to believe them. "Brownie will get you," we'd tell the younger kids, "She's an evil spirit, a baddie." By the look on their scared little faces, we knew they believed us. We made up rhymes and chanted them remorselessly, if ever she was forced to pass us. "Brownie, Brownie," we bayed, threateningly. "Brownie." We had no compassion.

On one occasion we tracked her home, staying far enough away not to alert her, or arouse the suspicions of any passing adults. She turned into a side street, and we followed at a distance. Then she sneaked down an alley, and we almost lost her, but for the clink of the key in the lock.

"Go on, I dare you!" One of the gang challenged me, looking me directly in the eye, and then down at the paving stone where a dog had conveniently parked its business. "Go on!" We managed to edge it onto a couple of chestnut leaves with a stick snapped from the hedge.

Once Brownie's door was firmly shut, I crept down the main path with the little bundle and was just about to post it through the letterbox when a voice thundered out, "Oy, you, what you doing?" A woman, grasping an alsatian by the collar, emerged from the adjoining door. "Get out of my garden, you little devil." I was stunned into inactivity for a second, but once I spotted the dog, tugging to get free, that was it. I let go of the offending parcel, turned tail, and fled. My mates had already scarpered. Was I ashamed? No, just glad the neighbour hadn't caught me, or unleashed the hound from hell.

Then, over time, Brownie dropped out of our lives. Most of us went on to secondary school, and some of us left the area entirely. We caught a different bus, arrived home earlier or later than before. We very rarely saw her. She was no longer a source of interest. She had become a nonentity, a mere blot on the landscape of our increasingly busy lives.

We forgot about her. That is, until the rumour went round that she had died. By this time we were all teenagers. The memories were catapulted into our consciousness.

We heard that she had died a millionaire.

The Census Taker
By Lou Storey

Cathy grips the holstered taser loosely as she nears the front door of the suburban split-level house. *Will I ever get used to this insanity?* Her steady refrain for this past year.

The Grays had appeared first. The colors came next, on the second and third days. Impossible circles materializing dead-center between the eyes, an area called the glabella. Hence the Glab, an inelegant moniker for these inexplicable, brilliantly-colored disks. Cathy's emerged on the second day. She had felt her Yellow Glab before ever seeing it. A feathery tickling across the eyebrows, accompanied by a clear-headed snap, like after a really good sneeze.

If someone had told Cathy back then that in a year she'd be doing exactly what she is doing right now, she'd have told them they were crazy.

Cathy presses the doorbell and waits as commotion accompanies the opening of the door. "Morensky family?" she asks.

"That's us! I'm Alison," a young woman cheerfully responds, holding back two rambunctious children. "Do you want to step in?"

Cathy frowns, steps back. *Step In and You Might Not Step Out.* The first rule of training.

"Oh, I'm so sorry, of course!" Alison says. "All these new rules, new everything."

Noting the Pink Glab, Cathy knows this woman is unlikely to lure her into danger, but the world is still sorting out the finer details of what traits accompany each color. Are all Pinks nurturing caregivers, all Greens loyal and trusting? Could a Blue be something other than sensitive or funny? The intuitive number-crunching Whites, the social butterfly and flighty Oranges . . . Cathy wondered, *Are we really this easy to typecast?* As a Yellow, Cathy is a lover of learning but holds some resentment that now artistic talent is solely a Purple trait, even if her talent remains latent. And Brights, what a mystery!

And Grays . . . Cathy stops, not wanting to go there. Besides, there could be one hiding behind the door right now, ready to leap out and . . .

"I want the lady to go away!" shouts the little tow-headed boy with the red circle between his eyes. Cathy and Alison laugh, easing the tension.

"And you must be Richard, Red, age seven," Cathy says, reading from her list. Reds are a handful. Cathy hopes for this mother's sake that there is plenty of activity to keep this little

Red busy. The other child Megan, Yellow, age six, and mother Alison, Pink, age thirty-five, all check out as registered.

"Your husband, and the Bright?" Cathy asks, "Sorry, I mean your younger son Samuel?"

Alison leans her head back for a full-throated yell, "Howard!"

Howard appears, holding an infant in his arms. He smiles and points helpfully to his Blue Glab, then crosses his eyes, triggering gales of delight from his children and an eye-roll from his wife.

"Everything here checking out?" he asks amiably. Cathy keeps her focus away from baby Samuel whose forehead beams like a flashlight. Even with her eyes averted, she can sense this creature's attention, touching, exploring. *Is this Bright in my head?*

Cathy is done here. Almost.

"One more thing. Are you harboring or know the whereabouts of any person or persons with a Gray Glab?" It would be easier to just say, "Seen any Grays?" but Cathy sticks to the script.

"I've only seen them on television," Alison says, "and this isn't that kind of neighborhood."

Cathy ignores the last comment, chalking it up to ignorance, and wishful thinking. "Lastly, are you aware of the code to dial to report a Gray, or to report any unusual or concerning events regarding Glab colorations?"

"1-0-1!" the entire family recites.

"Call 1-0-1 if a Gray's on the run!" the Red little boy sings out.

"We don't have to worry about that here, honey," Alison chides.

"That's all I need," Cathy says, her smile now a bit forced. *Even the nicest people can be so wrongheaded.*

NICE, a voice in her head whispers. Cathy pales, looks at the little creature held in his father's arms. *Are the Brights even human?* The baby's eyes are piercingly fixed on Cathy. *NICE*, he repeats, somewhere deep inside her.

"Thank you for participating in the Glab Census. And have a nice day." That last part is off-script, something Cathy does not normally say. The word *NICE* reverberates in her head. *Did he make me say that?*

Cathy walks briskly down the front yard's path leading to the sidewalk. She resists running, although she badly wants to get far away from baby Samuel. That poor woman, Cathy thinks. Brights are still a mystery. Most of the people who turned Bright last year during the three-day Reveal have since vanished, some within a few minutes, the longest lasting a handful of days, then just gone, and who knows where. Recent newborn Brights might eventually do the same but so far they remain.

NICE, the voice echoes again, even as Cathy is hurriedly turning the corner, the Morensky's house no longer in view.

Will I ever get used to this insanity? The whole topic of Grays confuses and upsets Cathy. Peter had done some bad things, true, but he could also be solicitous, charming, and smart. He had his dark moods, but who doesn't? Again, her thoughts are unwillingly returned to that awful morning – waking to find Peter sitting at the edge of their bed, bent fully forward. Over and over, that ungodly moan.

"What is it! What's wrong?" she'd said, catapulting herself to his side of the bed to switch on the light. Peter turned his head toward her. That's when she saw it, her first Gray. A shadowy irregular charcoal-gray marking that had not been there the night before, spread out in the space between his eyebrows.

"Are you in pain?" she asked, placing her hand protectively on the curious patch. Peter let out a scream at her touch. He pushed her away, struggling to stand, and made his way to the bathroom. Cathy joined him, both of them transfixed at the site of the curious marking on his forehead, painful to the touch, now milky-gray in the fluorescent light.

Peter was not alone. Large numbers of people were filling the emergency rooms at various hospitals. All sported similar gray, irregular-shaped markings in the same location. By late morning the Mystery Markings were appearing worldwide and especially in prisons. There was pressure for a government response, with scientists and national leaders stepping forward. Not until late evening of that first day did the President and Vice President of the United States televise an announcement, "There is no cause for alarm. Everything is under control." The reason for their delayed response was plain to see, sitting squarely between their eyes. It did not take long to figure out the qualities of a Gray.

Distant sirens save Cathy from the pain of remembering. A house across the street draws her attention. A pair of hands appear on the second-story windowsill and a heavy-set bald man comes into view. He's positioned awkwardly attempting to climb out the window, but he tumbles forward and flattens a hedge below. Rolling out of the greenery the man, his Glab of guilt evident, struggles to his feet and begins to run.

In less than a second Cathy crosses the street and takes aim, releasing her taser's high-volt web at the man's feet. He is stunned into a belly-flop, face down on his dandelion-studded lawn and hands over his head in surrender. His less-than-stellar escape is accompanied by an increasing volume of approaching sirens. Maintaining full attention on her capture, Cathy hears the slamming of car doors and the crackle of police monitors.

"Perp down!"

"Perp targeted!"

They love their job, Cathy thinks, relieved to be superfluous now.

Soon more guns are pointed at the prone Gray who is loudly crying, "Didn't do nothing! I didn't do nothing."

The SWAT team, a sea of Reds, busy themselves shouting orders while performing complex hand signals to each other as if expecting thousands of Grays to come tumbling out the windows and doors like some demented circus act. Cathy secures her weapon back into its holster and lets the real cops play cop.

Will I ever get used to this? Cathy wonders as she heads to her car. She calms herself with the thought of home, a nice shower, and her well-worn recliner waiting to be kicked back into the perfect seat next to a book eager to have its pages turned.

NICE, says a voice in her head.

No, I will never get used to this.

> *If only there were evil people somewhere*
> *insidiously committing evil deeds,*
> *and it were necessary only to separate them from*
> *the rest of us and destroy them.*
> *But the line dividing good and evil cuts through*
> *the heart of every human being.*
> *And who is willing to destroy a piece of his own heart?*

- Aleksandr Solzhenitsyn, (The Gulag Archipelago)

Betty's Boyfriend
By Anne Thomson

Betty Henderson is retching into the toilet bowl again. Kneeling on the faded linoleum, head hanging like a sick dog's, she tears off a piece of crisp toilet paper and dabs her mouth with it, wondering why they call it morning sickness when the crippling nausea lasts all day? She is thankful for her parents' long working hours, for how else would she manage to hide her symptoms?

Dizzy from rising too quickly, Betty shuffles unsteadily across the landing to her bedroom. She peers into the full-length mirror and is shocked by its reflection. Her face matches the shade of greasy white paint on her bedroom walls, she has a line of sweat on her top lip, and her hair is limp tails. She is meeting Maurice later. She must put her face on and make herself pretty because he doesn't know yet and today, she has decided, is the day she will tell him.

Stripping to her bra and pants, she stands sideways to the aged speckled silvered glass. Already, there is the suggestion of a paunch, as if she has eaten one too many helpings of pudding. Betty tries to imagine what she'll look like at six months but cannot imagine a full-blown pregnancy on her teenage body. How is it possible that her flat breasts will swell to the size of melons?

She steps into her favourite green polka dot dress, *may as well wear it while it still fits,* then drags a brush through her tangles. She and Maurice are in love. They will find rooms together. It will be just the three of them. Their own little family. Betty feels a warm surge for what is growing inside her.

***

"You and me forever, baby." That's what he had whispered in her ear while he fumbled with her knickers late at night in a dark corner of Bishop's Park, stuck his fingers up inside her, kissing her hard with his tongue. "Not yet, not here, Morrie." She wriggled free.

Each time she refused him, Maurice sulked, and refused to speak to her. One time, he turned plain nasty, and Betty grew frightened that she would lose him. And so it happened, finally, in an airless, smelly boarding house.

Maurice had arranged their day out. He had taken care of everything. Her boyfriend! So mature, eight years older than her, with a steady job at the garage. All of this attracted her to him. Betty had felt so grown-up, walking hand in hand with him.

They took the train to Brighton. The beach was packed with bodies and gay stripy deck chairs. They sat on the uncomfortable stones watching the waves until Maurice grew restless and took her to a crowded pub nearby. In its flower-filled garden Maurice encouraged her to try some ale and one of his cigarettes. To please him, she put her lips around the moist, flattened end and sucked hard. She spluttered and choked. Eyes watering, she passed it back to him and gulped her orange juice down.

Maurice slouched back on the bench, gloomily blowing smoke rings while Betty watched a solitary bee travel around the garden, pollinating as it went. Maurice was disappointed with her. She was too young, not sophisticated enough for him.

"I do love you Morrie," she whispered, and kissed his rough cheek. Later, on the promenade, he bought her a stick of rock and made her giggle with his saucy innuendos, and when she put the sweet stick inside her mouth his comment made her blush violently. But the hedonistic air of the seaside town packed with young lovers was working on her, and Betty, lightheaded with drink, became flirtatious, hanging on his arm, laughing at everything her boyfriend said. Daring now, she slid her free hand over his bottom and gave it a squeeze.

Time was racing. Mid-afternoon, and they had to catch the six-thirty train home. Betty wanted to go back to the beach and lie in the sun again, perhaps get an ice-cream, but Maurice wasn't in the mood for sunbathing.

"D'you love me, baby?"

"Of course, very much," she replied, solemnly.

He stuck his tongue inside her ear. Tingles, like tiny electric shocks, surged through her, and she grew damp. Grabbing Betty's hand, Maurice dragged her across the busy main road and up a narrow alley to a place where men slunk in doorways, drinking and smoking. Grubby buildings blocked out the sun and made Betty shiver. Maurice led her up three deep stone steps and pushed open the black door at the top. Inside, he spoke to a bored peroxide blonde who was filing her nails at the curved counter. She pushed a key at him.

The tiny room was stifling. It had a single bed, a narrow wardrobe, and a stained sink hanging off the wall. Clanking sounds rose from the floor.

"Boilers," said Maurice. "The boiler room must be below us."

Betty forced the sash window open and leant out to a view of the fire escape, to handrails covered in bird muck. How she longed for the shimmering sea. Hard to believe now that it was out there somewhere. Breathing deep, her lungs searched for the taste of salt air.

Maurice lay back on the bed and patted the counterpane. Betty left the window and sat beside him on the edge of the bed. He started nibbling her neck, her ears, working them alternatively with his tongue. Suddenly, he was on top of her, desperate, grinding himself painfully against her hip bone. She tried to slow him down, but he was undoing her blouse with determined fingers, managing the fastening of her bra expertly. The sudden sharp pain made Betty cry out, but soon she was moving with him, oblivious to the noise of the boilers and to the smell of bird shit. "Oh, I do love you," she gasped. "You're my all, you are, Morrie." They were halfway home on the train before Betty realised that Maurice hadn't said he loved her back.

* * *

Betty stumbles along the riverside path. People are staring but she doesn't care. When she told him he had turned pale.

"We'll sort it out," he said, looking past her.

Betty threw her arms around his neck. "We'll have to find rooms quickly. We could look this afternoon. I'll get the local paper." She smiled at his blank face. "To live, Morrie. I can't have the baby at home, can I?"

He pulled away, his eyes shrapnel. "You can't have it, full stop."

She began to cry. "I can't Morrie. Besides, those kinds of places . . . they're dirty . . . I could die. And it's ours. Our little baby. We love each other, don't we? What's so terrible about a little baby?"

"Silly tramp." Maurice spun back to face her. "Getting yourself knocked-up."

The worst part had been when he walked away. She hadn't followed, just watched him slouch off, hands in pockets, out through the park gate. Betty sways, gagging into her hands. She clutches the cold railings and stares out at the river. On the far side are two rowing boats. Their skimming action over the water distracts her momentarily, envious of the way they scud along so effortlessly. Then they too disappear, like Maurice, under the arches of Putney Bridge.

She sets off again, rocking unsteadily, heading towards a bench at the far end of the riverside walk where it is quiet, no people. She flops down onto the wooden seat and bends to remove her pumps. The tarmac is hot beneath her bare feet. For hours she sits, just watching the water. Betty thinks about praying. The church will be cool and dark, but she won't be welcome there.

She pictures her parents' faces when they find out and knows that she can't go home. Betty struggles with the zip of her dress, manages to loosen it and wriggles free. She pulls the straps of her bra down over her shoulders, tugs it around so that she can easily undo it, takes off her knickers. And she is naked. She makes a neat pile, folding her dress carefully and lays it over her underwear. On top of the pile, she places her pumps. The rails are cold on her bare flesh, but Betty doesn't notice as she climbs over, and stands hanging onto the wrong side of the railings, her fingers clutching onto the iron.

She leans forward, a ship's figurehead, and opens her hands. Clutching air, she releases herself, and her troubles, into the quick brown water. The current fingers the ribbon holding her ponytail, undoes it, and her hair streams like weed. Her face is skyward, her arms pulling like oars, and she is a sleek vessel, untethered.

A Good Report
By Graham Steed

Imagine this . . . a body on the tideline. Right by my deckchair spot. A woman's body. I'm annoyed. Now I must trudge back up the hill and phone 999.

Hello. I'm Norman. I've just found a body in Smugglers Cove.

Yes. It's near the monastery.

No. Not accessible by vehicle.

I live on the hill. On sunny days I bring my deckchair down.

. . . She must have floated in on the tide.

The body is on the tideline. High water at 15:06.

Perhaps she rolled in on the last high water twelve hours ago. Perhaps she came for a swim and drowned – how many ways can a person die?

Do you recognise her?

   I can't see her face.

You live on the hill?

   Yes.

It's quite a way to the nearest town.

11 miles

Who else uses this beach? Surfers? Anglers? Dog walkers?

Few people come this way, Inspector.

Motorboats, dinghies with outboards? Heard any of those, sir?

No, Sergeant. The locals say the Germans landed an agent here from a submarine. Been rather quiet since.

Do you work, Norman?

I am retired.

You are a bit young to be retired.

I inherited the house and money, Inspector.

And before that?

I was a Master Mariner and lately a pilot for the river.

So, you know the waters round here.

Yes.

You have knowledge of the tides, currents . . .

Certainly.

Are you married?

No, never got round to it.

Notice any road traffic last night, sir, or early this morning?

Nothing out of the usual, Sergeant. If you ask me, she floated in on the tide.

Check with the coastguard, Sergeant. Good place for smugglers. Thus, the name. You will have to leave the beach, Norman. The duty pathologist and forensics will be here soon. The beach will be off limits until we have finished.

The murder squad telling me I must leave my beach?

No way.

If you have observed me from the cliff top, you will see I have not moved. Called nobody, spoken to nobody - except to the voices in my head. You have also noticed the cloud shadows sailing across the beach, and out at sea are grey swells turning silver in the sunbeams. Then you'll see me setting out my deckchair, and sitting, pondering.

Who was this person lying so still on my beach? She has a name. Death ends a life, a marriage even, but not a name. That stays forever. She has or had a father and mother, sisters and brothers perhaps.

There is a ring catching sunlight on her hand, so maybe a partner. Did he or she love her, and she in return? Were there children? Nothing new under the sun, so I am suddenly reminded of Hannah, a wife to Elkanah. He had another wife, Peninnah, who had children, but Hannah did not bear him so many children, yet it was Hannah whom Elkanah loved. What is it in a woman that brings love to a man's heart?

I dare now to look at the body. It lies not three metres from the incoming tide. I am in no doubt she is dead, for the dead lie differently from the sleeper. The dead are frozen in attitude, vacant; they lie in bad places, bring fascination or horror to the viewer, they float . . .

I rose and took a few steps nearer the body. What of her last moments? Did she know she would not, *could* not survive? Did she die of natural causes, or was she murdered?

She is dressed in casual wear: jeans and a short black top which shows her midriff. Her shoes or sandals are missing. She lies face down, but even in death there is a lustre to her short, black hair.

The high tide laps at her body. I believe she floated in some twelve hours ago, borne in on rising water during matins when monks rise and pray by candlelight *Venite adoremus*.

She should have a proper burial or cremation, her body treated with dignity – not the indignity of lying on a pathologist's slab, of being photographed before her clothes are cut away, of shears crunching her ribs apart so as to expose her bewildered heart: everything outside and inside the body must be examined, and in the case of this young woman a further question – was she pregnant?

All I must do is to call 999 to begin the grisly process.

But, as you can see from the hilltop, I hesitate . . .

If you are still on the hilltop, you can see the town away to the north west. With binoculars you make out the river entrance, perhaps a ferry inward or outward-bound in the channel. You may see a light aircraft or helicopter rising above the town skyline from the nearby airfield; a helicopter can sweep over the coves and bays, catch me dithering, caught between Do and Do Not.

I need a good report, you see. I will not say too much, but I know the inside of a crown court, a prison van and a prison cell where I spent eight weeks. What did General Grant say to a soldier brought before him, "Don't worry, boy, you'll get justice here." And the soldier replied, "That's what I'm afraid of, General." Likewise, I have a thing about justice.

Since my 'experience' I fear that in any future time that I'm weighed in the balance I'll be found wanting, like Belshazzar. Everything I say will be taken down and used in evidence against me.

Justice must seek out the bad, punish the good . . .

I want you to attend a voluntary interview at the police station, Norman. You are not under arrest, but you will be under caution.

How can I refuse?

You may have a legal representative.

Of course. The more people who see my reasonableness, my co-operation, my desire to be open and honest, the more will give me a good report.

Except every good point will be offset by a single bad point: me alone on a beach with a body.

It is not for our sins we are punished, but for our crimes.

* * *

Over my swimming trunks I am wearing a cream and white striped bathrobe. I lay the robe on my deckchair, pull out the tie cord and fashion a harness. The tide paws at the corpse as if to wake it. I stand astride the body, slip the harness over the feet and work it up the body to the armpits. My plan is to tow the body out into deeper water, then release it to the currents.

It's not like launching a boat: with a push the bow rises

to the waves, the craft surges forward, we clamber aboard and ship the rudder.

But a body is lumpen, not built for the sea. I haul it into the shallow breakers. When I strain, the water against my back is cold and punchy. It tries pushing me against the body. When I strain again, my feet slip. Cloudy sea water smothers my face and fills my ears and mouth.

I hear muffled sounds of legs kicking. When I rise, my eyes are gummed by salt. I feel my belly cringing, my mouth straining to vomit. I yank the harness in panic. The hard bone skull crashes against my nose, but I grab it and hang on, drifting along in a daze – a live head resting on a dead head. When I find the energy to wipe blood and salt from my eyes, I see the cliff line. Not much progress so far, but now the tide should be ebbing.

I make better progress when I adjust the harness. Now I can swim breaststroke with the body lying on my back.

Have you noticed how the temperature chills as you go further out, or how the sea hums in deeper water? Perhaps it is the ocean's deep dynamos or the murmuration of Poseidon himself. Perhaps it's water on my ear drums.

* * *

Am I heavy?
    Only a little.
How far are you taking me?
    Where you came from.

I am not from the sea.

> *You were washed up.*

I was trying to escape.

> *Who from?*

From you . . .

I can swim no further. I let the body slip away. I turn for the shore. I'm cold. The tide is ebbing. It'll be a tough swim back.

You've left me.

> *I had to.*

I doted on you.

> *I couldn't handle it.*

I'm lonely.

> *So am I.*

We could have worked it out.

> *You'll always be my true love.*

And you mine.

Only when I stagger out of the water do I realise I have left my bathrobe harness attached to the body.

* * *

I'm up early. I run to the hilltop. The beach is clear. I scour the water with binoculars. The sea is clear. My tense shoulders sink in relief. I think I am breathing. I wave to the helicopter passing over . . .

A Mother's Love
By Sue Buckingham

"Hi, Mum."

"Is that Jane?"

"Yes, Mum," I replied wearily. Who did she think it was? She had rung my mobile number; Mandy was dead and Mark didn't speak to her – who else could it be?

Of course, I then felt bad for even thinking this. She came from an era of ringing a landline, where any member of the family might answer. Mind you, even if I had a landline for her to ring, no-one else was going to answer, there was only me.

There was only me.

A bolt of loneliness shot through me, and then despair.

There was only me.

Only me, to pay all the bills; the mortgage, the credit card, the utilities. Only me, to cook and clean, for only me. Only me, sat in front of the telly, late at night, not wanting to go to bed because there was only going to be me in it. Only me, to get up in the morning, eat a solitary breakfast and then go to work to try and earn enough money to pay all the bills; the mortgage . . .

Only me, to answer the phone to my mother and dread what this call might be about.

"Who's Mark?"

I thought I must have misheard her.

"Who's Mark?" I repeated back, like some sort of parrot.

"Yes, that's what I said. Who's Mark?" Her voice was querulous, but I could also hear an undercurrent of fear.

I wasn't sure how to reply. She should know that Mark was her son, but clearly she didn't. Unless, of course, she meant someone else called Mark. Her window cleaner? Someone trying to sell her new double glazing? One of her neighbours? If I told her she had a son called Mark, she might think I was patronising her and get upset. Alternatively, she might genuinely have forgotten she had a son called Mark and then I would be really concerned.

"I'm not sure, Mum," I said hesitantly. "Which Mark are you talking about?" This seemed like a safe option.

"I don't know. That's why I'm asking you." Now there was definite anger there.

"Well, what is making you ask me who Mark is? Is he someone who has called at the door?"

"I don't think so."

"You're going to have to give me a bit more than that, Mum. Is he someone from your past that you've been thinking about?'

"Yes, that's it!" She sounded much happier now. But this only served to make me more concerned. It did feel like she had forgotten her only son.

I tried to be tactful. "Maybe you've been thinking about my brother Mark?"

"Have you got a brother called Mark then, dear?"

This was really worrying.

"I tell you what, Mum, why don't I pop over and we can have a cup of tea and a chat together?"

"You don't need to do that," her voice was harsh. "All you need to do, is tell me who Mark is and if he's your brother. I don't know why you have to keep all these secrets from me, all the time. You always were a secretive little girl and you've not changed one bit as you've got older. Frankly, I'm getting fed up with it all." She was shouting now.

"Mum, I'm on my way. I'll see you in ten minutes and we can talk about it then." I ended the call and grabbed a coat and my car keys.

Arriving in her street, I did a quick turn in the road and found an empty space just a few doors away from her house. Lights were streaming from every window. I parked and almost ran down the pavement. What was going on in there? Was she having a party with this so-called Mark who she couldn't remember? Had she invited some stranger in off the street and offered him the use of her bathroom and spare bedroom?

I was being ridiculous – she had probably just forgotten to

turn the lights off when she left each room. And if I arrived red-faced and out of breath, she might not know who I was, panic and call for the police.

I slowed down, took two or three deep breaths and actively relaxed all my body. Mum had just had a 'moment' and she would be fine. Feeling better, I knocked on the door.

Although it was nine o'clock at night and dark outside, she opened the door without querying who was at the door, or using the safety chain. Two simple checks I had tried to drum into her.

"Oh, hello, love," she said. "What a lovely surprise to see you. It's not very nice out there. Come on in and we can have a cup of tea."

The composure I had built up on the doorstep evaporated. I barked, "Mum! How many times do I have to tell you to put the chain on the door before you open it?"

She stepped back in alarm and nearly fell over. I managed to reach in and grab her, just about keeping her on her feet.

"Ow, Ow!" she shouted in shock and pain. My grip was tight on her bony wrists, thin and fragile under my fingers. I leaned forward and awkwardly shifted my position, letting go of her wrists and placing my arms around her back. Now I had her in a bear hug and she started to struggle against me.

"Help," she whimpered. "Somebody, please help me."

"Mum, it's me, Jane. You're okay."

"Help me, someone." Her voice was a bit louder now.

The front door was still open behind me and all I needed now was a diligent Neighbourhood Watch member phoning the police.

"Mum, please, it's me. Your daughter. Jane. I'm not going to hurt you. I'm just trying to make sure you aren't going to fall."

Her head dropped until it was nestled into my shoulder. She stopped struggling and started to weep quietly. I gently manoeuvred her around and into the living room. By now, she was grasping hold of me as if she were drowning and the weeping had turned into low-pitched keening.

I managed to settle her into her chair and leaned over her, hugging her gently and murmuring over and over, "You're alright. Everything's going to be fine. Don't cry, Mum. Please don't cry."

I felt like crying myself. I really didn't need this. It felt as if I was the mother and Mum was my child. A single mother at that. No-one to help me. All the responsibility on my shoulders. Only me, making all the decisions, good and bad.

I straightened up, my back cricking as the bones settled back into place.

"Are you okay now?"

"Yes, I think so. Thank you for coming to my rescue, I don't know what would have happened if you hadn't been here."

She seemed to have completely forgotten that she had rung me earlier and so I took the coward's way out.

"That's okay. It's all over now. Shall we have a cup of tea?"

"Oh, yes please, that would be lovely. Are you going to make me some dinner? I haven't eaten yet today, but suddenly I'm starving."

I made her some beans on toast and chatted away to her while she ate. I kept clear of the subject of Mark, security chains or anything else I thought might upset her, or me.

It was close to ten o'clock by the time she had finished her meal and drunk three cups of tea, so I helped her up to bed.

"Goodnight, my darling," she said as I tucked her in. "Thank you so much for coming over. I get so lonely on my own. It's really lovely to have company. Especially the company of my beautiful daughter. I do love you, Amanda."

My eyes instantly filled with tears and I had to turn away. I said quietly, "Mum, I'm Jane."

"Yes, of course you are. That's what I said. I do love you, Jane."

"I love you too, Mum."

You Sent Me Flowers
By David Higham

You sent me flowers I did not want. *To Julia* was all it said on the card. I really did not care about you that much. They were a nuisance, I thought. I did not want the attention, Giles.

You had chosen well. You had not sent red roses; you would not be that obvious. The flowers were unusual. Had you taken time to choose them – or just left it to the florist? I did not know the names of most of them. Some of them seemed to be wild flowers. I could not help but bury my nose in your bouquet. You had sent me scents of spring, of meadows and of honey.

I breathed them in again. Had you imagined me with my nose buried deep in the bouquet?

I pulled myself together; after all, they came from you. I just wasn't that interested. I wanted nothing from you. I went to my compost bin to dispose of them — and you. I turned away from the bin, the flowers still in my hand. I turned away from the thought of you and reached for a vase.

Had you seen me doing that, arranging your flowers in a vase?

They lasted well, the flowers, but so did unwanted thoughts of you. As blooms faded I removed them, snipping away at the image of you in my head. There was a sachet of plant reviver. *Use this product on the third day,* the label read. It would be a waste not to use it, I thought, this extension to your gift. The flowers revived, as did unbidden feelings about you. I got used to having them around, the flowers that is; maybe the thoughts as well. Had you been thinking of me?

The flowers lasted a week. I was surprised by a sense of regret when they finally died.

You had not followed up with a message or a phone call, so into the bin went you and your flowers. I felt a sense of relief not to be reminded of you. I felt free but vaguely discontented.

Was I missing you? Not really, just curiosity.

Were the flowers a farewell?

Had you moved on from me? Did I mind?

That was last Tuesday.

Today there is a click and a flop at the front door. More flyers, I think, no one sends me snail mail; but you had. I pick up the envelope. You had addressed it to me with a fountain pen on good paper in a firm, confident hand. I open the tissue-lined envelope. You had written on crisp, linen paper. Good grief, you are wooing me. Nobody woos nowadays. It feels intriguing, strangely good.

I fetch a glass of wine; find a comfortable chair by the window in the sun. I sit down, draw my legs up under me and, only now, I start to read your letter.

The Reception
By Ian Inglis

After a gap of many years, I'm invited to weddings again. As a young man, of course, there were always plenty to go to. We – I include myself – seemed to be in a race, a contest to make public the transition into independent adulthood, and getting married was a first step on that journey. Now, when I look back at those days, I'm reminded how inexperienced, how unworldly, how ill-prepared we all were. What were we thinking of? Why were we in such a rush?

Unsurprisingly, many of those early marriages failed. Mine, for example. Fortunately, Susan and I realised our mistake within a couple of years, and parted before we could inflict any lasting harm on each other. But others of our friends chose to doggedly cling on, like exhausted tennis players facing an inevitable defeat, pointlessly hitting the ball backwards and forwards over an unforgiving net.

What I find truly astonishing is that after surviving such a harrowing experience, the majority of those men and women –

now in their forties and fifties, even their sixties – should decide to do it all over again. But they do. They do. And those are the people to whose weddings – lavish, sophisticated, tasteful affairs – I now find myself invited. One of them is my brother, Raymond. And I'm here at his wedding, his third, today. I'm the best man.

Raymond is sixty – a couple of years older than myself. His bride is Margaret, who's at least twenty years younger. I have to say he's quite a catch. He's the CEO of a financial services institution whose primary function – so far as I can understand it – is to enable credit-card companies to engage in international transactions at minimal cost, and he is very wealthy. Despite the demands of two ex-wives, Raymond remains a very wealthy man; indeed, he seems to become wealthier every time I see him.

Which isn't very often. Which is why I don't know many of the guests here today. And they don't know me. A few of them might recognise my name. Nicholas Froome. I'm a writer. I've produced two novels: *Clay Lake*, which was a critical and commercial success; and *Gleeman*, which was not. My third, *The Apothecary*, has been meandering along for the past five years like a sluggish river. But it's finally arrived at its destination, and will be in the shops later this year. My publisher, my editor, my literary agent, and early reviewers all seem to have high hopes for it. Well, they would, wouldn't they? When I read it, I notice defects.

And here we are at this splendidly-restored Georgian mansion, in several acres of parkland. I'm told it's a very popular, and very expensive, wedding venue. The service is scheduled for one o'clock, followed by a grand luncheon in the afternoon, and dancing in the evening. A marquee. Fireworks. Numerous buffet opportunities. Carriages at midnight. But before all that, there's the pre-wedding champagne reception. And the guests - at least 150 of them - are already here, meeting, greeting, conversing, rehearsing, mingling, tingling with excitement. It's quite an occasion. We're just waiting for Raymond and Margaret to arrive, and then the ceremony itself can begin.

I wander around, among these people with whom I have very little in common. I see a clutch of bullish men standing silently in a circle in the centre of the room, slyly appreciating the trim figures of the waitresses, while their elegant wives casually look around for the handsome stranger they saw in the entrance hall.

In a corner by an open window, an unusually pale man with rapidly receding hair is talking earnestly to a young woman. "The moment of extinction is as important as the moment of creation," I hear him say. She holds her face so tightly that I fear it will collapse if her concentration falters.

I move closer to a group of middle-aged men sharing a joke. "Oh, you're right there," one hoots. "In my day, sex was something you did to a woman, rather than with her. And you had to work damned hard to persuade her to let you do it!" His friends roar with laughter.

Three women move closer together, and scrutinise me suspiciously as I pass. "I've always said that," the first one confides. "He listens, but he doesn't hear; he looks, but he doesn't see; he talks, but he doesn't say anything."

"That's exactly how I would have put it," the second woman agrees. "Absolutely," says the third.

I return to the centre of the room, where one of the bullish men is holding an unlit cigar in his hand. I tap him on the shoulder. "No smoking," I remind him. He stares at me in disbelief.

So, these are my brother's, and my soon-to-be sister-in-law's, friends. I find myself wondering again why he has chosen me as his best man. Or why he's invited me here at all. We're not close. Not in the way brothers are supposed to be. Perhaps it's because I'm his only living relative.

His two previous marriages produced no children – I've never asked if that was by choice – and although I'd struggle to properly explain it, I understand that the idea of family, however fractured or distorted or incomplete that may be, is one of the few constants in all our lives. And I'm grateful to him. But I still wonder why I'm here.

I step out on to the patio and gaze across to the line of hills in the distance – 'those blue remembered hills' that Housman described – and suddenly Raymond is there by my side. Perhaps he's been out here all the time, or perhaps he's been closeted in a side room, waiting to make his entrance.

"Nick," he says, shaking my hand. "Nick, it's good to see you. You're looking well."

"Ray. Your big day. Nervous?"

"No," he laughs. "Why should I be? I've done this twice before, you know!"

"Third time lucky?" I risk.

"Something like that."

"All these people . . . who are they?"

"I know, I know," he replies, catching my meaning. "They're alright. Well, most of them."

"Margaret? Is she here yet?"

"On her way, apparently. No rush." He laughs again. "Your speech?"

"Yes," I say. "Short and sweet."

"Quality not quantity, eh? Mine's the other way round. Just watch! The minute I get up to speak, people will start to nod off. At least, they will if they've got any sense! I wish I was more like you, good with words. Numbers, stats, tech – yes. Words – no. Which reminds me: *The Apothecary*. Will I like it? Will I understand it?"

"How did you hear . . ." I begin.

"You think I don't keep up with your work? I show off to people all the time: Yes, that Nicholas Froome. The novelist. My brother."

A black Bentley sweeps past us on the gravelled drive.

"They're here sooner than I thought," he says. "Come on, we'd better go inside."

The room I left a few minutes earlier has been transformed. Rows of velvet-covered chairs have appeared from somewhere, and the guests are starting to take their places. Raymond and I make our way to the front of the room and stand side-by-side at the head of the aisle. I hear the opening chords of Wagner's Bridal March. He turns to me.

"Got the ring?"

I touch my jacket pocket.

"Yes."

He takes a deep breath.

"Here we go, then."

"Good luck," I say.

He nods, happiness and excitement spreading across his face. His optimism, his confidence, are infectious and as Margaret walks slowly towards him, I find myself smiling with them both and begin to understand why he asked me to be his best man.

A Bad Hair Day
By Susan R Barclay

I'm sitting in a New York city restaurant, having a bad hair day, and waiting on my ex-lover. I didn't particularly want to come; who has the time? I feel like a one-armed juggler (as my dad used to say when he meant a one-armed wallpaper hanger) with way too many things to do. But I lost a bet with my Wiccan friend. Plus, I'm always down for a dare.

I run my thumb across the dull chip in the wine glass, thinking about this ex-lover, who used to be an architect before he discovered he loved OxyContin more than he loved designing buildings. He was an okay guy, I guess, even though he was way too much into Billie Eilish.

That was one of our problems. Well, besides the OxyContin. The attention he gave Eilish irked me. I mean, I'm no saint (sure as hell ain't a preacher's daughter or a nun), and I sure as hell can't sing, but certainly he understood my need for his attention.

The barista grinds her coffee beans behind the bar, which

holds several bowls of peanuts for the customers and a separate bowl of sliced lemons that appear to be from the night before. She's dressed like a short-order cook, which confuses me; she seems out of place here. Then again, I've had the coffee here and there's no mistaking the similarity between it and the sludge served in many diners across this city. Later, as a new and younger crowd fills the space, she'll grind the juice machine instead.

I'm taking advantage of the wi-fi in this shipwreck of a place, searching on my phone for my local polling place for the upcoming election, when there he is. Standing at my table like a cartoon character positioned in the wrong cel. His clothing reminds me of a mismatched Rubik's cube: no symmetry, no matching, no nothing. Just a conglomeration of colors that are sliding perpetually into a mud puddle after a broken friendship. Like ours.

" 'Sup?" he conjures.

I can see he's been to the orthodontist; he has braces now. I wonder if he found the money for those by selling the Ritalin or the Ambien. Either way, I know he's on something. His frog-like voice and his mummified state tell me all I need to know: he's on something.

I leaned upon a functional lie my parents used to tell about their rollercoaster of a marriage – just like a metronome swinging back and forth in perfect rhythm, fluctuating between the coldness of snow days and the heat and damage of summer hail storms. I tell him I'm doing just fine, and I can hear the choir of cicadas playing repeatedly in my head, much like a bad 90s hip hop song: *liar, liar, pants on fire; you are a mummy roasting on a pyre.* They knew I lied; would he?

Truth was, I missed him. We had met at the wedding of a mutual friend. The bandage across his nose had caught my attention. Well, that and his alien gray skin tone. That should have been my first clue of what a rite of passage with him would entail. But love has a way of blinding the most astute of souls. No; at that moment, and for the next few months, we entered our chess game of trying to make us work. I didn't count on Eilish and containers of pills. But there were good times and, especially, the sex. Oh God! The sex was good. Maybe that's what I missed so terribly; not him, but the sex. It has been a while for me.

I explained I had called him on a whim; I was thinking about him (I didn't tell him I was thinking about him because of the Wiccan-friend dare) and I wanted to see how he was doing. He rattled off some story about an ex-pet, traffic cones and Sasquatch and thanked me for thinking of him. Or, and by the way, did I have a few dollars I could toss his way? Of course, I did; I always did.

I dug through my purse, past the bank statement indicating a dangerously-low account balance, past a couple of stray matchsticks from the boxes I'd slid in my bag when the barista was distracted, and past the old Valentine's card I wish would have been from him. I handed over the few dollars I had. Upon which he bent low, placed his orthodontics-filled mouth against my cheek and kissed me, before turning and walking out.

I'm sitting in a New York city restaurant, having a bad hair day, and watching my ex-lover leave. I didn't particularly want to come; I have way too many things I should be doing. But I lost a bet with my Wiccan friend. I lost a lover and a few dollars, too.

Cold Hands and Bananas
By Gwenda Major

Late November and the first really cold day of winter. White frost on the grass. Car windscreens laced with ice. A bright blue cloudless sky.

I was walking along a woodland path through layers of fallen leaves softened by the recent rains. The strobing effect of light filtering between the trees made it hard to see ahead. My breath hung ghostly in front of me.

The only people about were a couple of dog walkers. We smiled a greeting. I'd forgotten to bring my gloves and my fingers were nipping with the cold, forcing me to stick my hands into my pockets.

Was that what triggered the memory?

***

I'm nine years old and standing at a bus stop after my piano lesson. I'm on my way back to the village and the Saturday ritual of tea at my best friend's house.

As usual, I haven't enjoyed the piano lesson. My teacher

Mr Gillow is creepy, stands behind me to reach over my shoulders to the piano keys. Offers me a square of Cadbury's Dairy Milk at the end of each lesson which I feel I have to accept. I don't like his dog either, a bull terrier with bow legs who stares at me with his pink eyes when I'm playing *Für Elise*.

It's chilly and I wish the bus would hurry up. My hands are cold and I've forgotten my gloves. I open and close my fingers over and over again to stop the nipping. I'm hoping Carol's mum has made ham sandwiches for tea. I always like her sandwiches, the way she removes the crusts and cuts them into little triangles. Sometimes we have jelly for pudding and then we watch television before Carol's dad walks me back home.

A car pulls up in front of me, a big silver car. I can see there are two people sitting in the front.

The window nearest to me is wound down. A woman smiles at me and says, "Where are you heading, dear?"

Have I been warned about not talking to strangers? "I'm going to my friend's for tea in the village," I say.

"In Westerthorpe?" the woman asks. Her voice is friendly, concerned.

"Yes – she lives at Garthdale Crescent."

"Hop in then dear. We'll give you a lift. It's too cold to be standing out here for long, isn't it?"

Do I hesitate? I'm used to doing what grown-ups tell me to do.

The woman reaches around and opens the back door and

I slide in and place my leather music case neatly on the seat beside me. It's nice and warm in the car and there's a lemony smell of polish.

I hope I won't feel car sick. My dad hates it when I feel sick and he has to stop and let me out to vomit by the roadside. The car pulls smoothly away from the kerb. It's very comfortable and definitely quieter than our car. I watch the trees and fields drift by. My fingers are starting to feel better now.

The man has dark hair and is wearing a sheepskin coat like my dad's. I can't see his face, only his hands resting on the steering wheel.

The woman's head disappears for a moment and then she half leans around in her seat. She's holding something out to me.

"Would you like a banana?" she asks.

For a moment I don't know what to do. I've always hated bananas: the smell, the texture, the taste of them. But I know it would be rude to refuse, so I take the fruit and say, "Thank you." I look at it and take a deep breath. Then I peel the skin back and shut my eyes as I take a first bite of the soft flesh. I have to force myself to swallow so I finish the whole banana in three bites to get it over with. It's a relief when it's all gone. Now the car smells of banana instead of lemons and I wish I could open the window to let some fresh air in, but I daren't.

It's not really far to my village and I can see that this is where I would be standing up and ringing the bell if I was on the bus. Now I wish I was on the bus.

The man and the woman are murmuring to each other in the front seat. I can't hear any words because of the noise of the engine.

Just before the church the man pulls into a lay-by and the woman says, "Will you be all right from here? We turn off after this."

"Yes, that's okay," I say. I fumble with the car door.

"Can you manage?" the woman says.

"Yes, I'm okay." I twist myself out of the car, almost forgetting my music case and then I carefully shut the door. The woman gives me a little wave through her open window.

"Thank you," I remember to say.

"That's alright. Take care now," she says and winds the window up again. The car pulls away and I watch it turn towards the coast and disappear.

I realise I'm still holding the banana skin in my hand. I make sure nobody is watching and then I drop it in the long grass by the roadside, wiping my hands on my skirt. I look both ways and cross over to walk to Carol's house.

***

A couple of weeks later I hear Mum and Grandma talking in low voices.

"Those poor parents. You'd never get over something like that would you?"

"It's your worst nightmare. You daren't let your children

out of your sight these days."

"I hope they catch them and throw away the key."

Soon everyone is talking about it. A girl almost my age was seen getting into a car. The witness said there were two people inside, a man and a woman. A few days later they found the girl's body in woodland not far from the village.

I haven't told anyone about the lift I accepted in the silver car - and now I can't. I know my parents would be angry with me.

And there's something else, a question that keeps running around in my head. Why did they choose her? Why wasn't it me?

The Edge
By Gillian Brown

The surgery lights glare with hyper-intensity tonight. Sweat drips from your brow. You glance at your watch: 9 pm. The air-con switched off an hour ago, that's why it's stifling hot. A mosquito whines past your ear. You swat it and miss. Another failure to add to the list.

Your phone beeps. You squeeze your eyes shut. That will be Anna. You're late. You're always late.

Vince? There is no need for more. You've known each other long enough.

On my way, you tap back.

Her interruption kills off your last shred of concentration, as intended. She's right. It's late. Exhaustion rushes in like a tsunami, smashing everything in its path except for your storm-proof anxiety. Anna will have cooked dinner. You're not hungry. Young Luca will be waiting to see you before he goes to bed. Tomorrow is a school day.

You grab some paperwork and stuff it in your briefcase.

Doctors are trained to leave their work behind in the surgery. Mentally as much as physically. Easier said than done. You sigh, pull the papers out again and lock them in the top drawer. But the self-doubt and guilt remain. You're too drained to rationalise why.

Since your last patient left at six, you have been caught up in what your son calls Google mania. Researching this disease and that. Checking out the latest scientific findings. Examining why a patient doesn't respond to a certain drug. Why another suffers an adverse effect. Is it your fault? The question-mark grows bigger every day.

Admittedly, you care less and less, which is alarming. Patients surge in with the slightest symptom these days, usually after their own obsessive online research. Your patience is dwindling. Minor ailments cannot be cured with a simple prescription anymore. A kind word and a smile have little or no effect. Your patients' anxieties become your anxieties. Each day they tower higher and higher until your sanity threatens to topple.

The phone beeps again. *V?*

Coming.

You swallow hard, dreading the thought of returning to these four square walls in a few hours' time, with your brain still shredded after another sleepless night. A sadness drags across the pit of your stomach as you remember how you once loved this job. It was your childhood dream come true. Not long ago, it brought fulfilment and pleasure. What went wrong? God, how you've tried to get the feeling back.

Once you get home, Anna heats up pasta in the microwave. Luca wanders into the kitchen wearing his Tyrannosaurus pyjamas and a crooked smile. "Goodnight, Dad," he says and slouches off.

You jump up, twirl him around and give him a hug. It's not enough. You both know it. You and Anna eat in silence, neither enjoying the meal.

You squeeze out a smile. "Delicious!"

She gives you a look – a mix of empathy and frustration. You know what's coming. "You're not doing your patients any favours by overworking like this." She places her fists on the table and looks you straight in the eye. "My love. This must stop." Perhaps to soften her ultimatum, she gets up and plants a kiss on your cheek from behind. Her lips are warm on your lifeless skin.

School holidays arrive. You arrange for a week off work to treat Anna and Luca to a break in the Alps. You owe them that.

"Mont Blanc," you say. "Mountain bikes. Big challenges. Spectacular scenery. You'll both love it."

"I'm sure we will. But it's you I'm worried about, Vince," Anna says. "What about going to a spa or taking a beach holiday? Relax. Luca can do water sports. You need some 'me' time. Body and soul. Let yourself be spoiled and pampered, without commitments."

Relax? The word sounds like a distant memory. "I'll be

fine," you say, the doubt churning inside.

Anna knows better than to insist. But after a day in the Alps, she is proved right. Instead of a gentle bike ride, you opt for a gruelling climb. You push yourself to the limits and achieve nothing but pain and self-loathing. Your body reacts like a bag of broken bones. Your muscles ache. Worn out and hating yourself for it, you hide behind a mask that both Anna and Luca see through. It's a relief for all the family when the week is up and it is time to go home.

The first morning back at work, a sudden dizziness fills your head. Your assistant insists on taking you home. She leads you through a waiting room full of expectant patients. Your apologetic smile does nothing to deter the dropped jaws and worried whispers.

Anna has to force you to stay home and rest. "They've found a replacement for a month," she says. You feel as small as a microbe, but with none of its benefits.

One month turns into six. Then a year. Your life is programmed. Cognitive therapies. Sleep treatment. Stress management. Specialists patch your mental wounds and mend the cracks. There seems no end to it. You've had enough. You insist that you are okay. Finally, it is decided you are fit to resume your practice.

On the first day back, you stop the car some distance from the surgery, take a deep breath and grip the steering wheel. Your knuckles whiten. Are you ready for this? So soon? The answers battle it out. Yes. No. Perhaps. Old wounds open up. The shame of having let everyone down squirms like a worm inside your chest. Before anyone spots your car, you spin the wheel round and drive off.

Anna isn't going into work today. Perhaps she guessed this might happen. But you don't head for home. You drive out to the clifftops.

Far below, the ocean froths and roars. One simple jump and the waves would smash you against the rocks, then suck you out to sea. Its indifference is inviting. As is the resulting void.

But this was never your plan. Your easy access to barbiturates would be a better choice. But still.

The sea snarls. Your heart thunders. Through all this, the screech of a seagull chick reaches you, rising up from over the edge of the cliff. Its desperate cry touches every nerve in your body. Is it hungry? Or, is it in danger of falling out of its nest and plummeting to its death? Within seconds, its mother arrives and swoops down towards it.

An image of Luca flashes before you. He should be at school but he is still in his pyjamas. *Where's Dad?* he repeats over and over. Anna drops her head in her hands. She has no tears left. Nor words. Behind your wife and son, a line of patients stretches into the distance. Their expressions are resigned but you sense their desperation.

A sudden sound distracts you. Happy chirps fly up, breaking

through the ocean's roar. The chick's sheer joy at being alive touches your soul. You step back from the edge and return the way you've come.

Ms Molly Gets Herself Noticed
By Maggie Sinclair

The clubhouse doesn't look much from the outside, a big grey building, no windows, no signs. It's what's inside that interests Molly. She knows she shouldn't be walking here alone at night. She's been told often enough, but what's the worst that can happen? The steady beat of too-loud music vibrates through the walls. No girls allowed. Molly grins, imagining the boys lounging at the pool table, swigging beer from the bottle and exchanging abusive pleasantries.

Outside the building stands a row of highly-polished, high-powered machines, neat and tidy, unlike their owners. *Like dominoes,* thinks Molly. A figure emerges and slouches against the wall rolling a cigarette, long hair and dirty denim.

Not a bit like James; he was so handsome in his white t-shirt, hair slicked back. He thought he was a real hero on his Vincent Black Lightning. Young Molly thought so too. Well, every girl loves a bad boy. Molly was a good girl though, invisible to the wonderful James. She couldn't compete with the wild girls from the convent school. *He was so arrogant.*

The scruffy figure stamps out his cigarette and disappears back inside. Molly emerges from the shadows and studies the line of shiny bikes. They look heavy, but she knows what to do. Lean in hard, lift the side-stand, and . . .

With the crash of metal on metal echoing through the night, the doors burst open to disgorge a black-leathered rabble, muscles flexed, ready to meet a crowbar-brandishing rival gang. They stand bewildered in the empty street and stare after the little old lady as she limps into the darkness.

Perfect Rows of Little Squares
By Maureen Cullen

I walk through the park, my senses flooding with sweet scent from planted beds. My muscles loosen, my neck eases and my shoulders relax under the sun's warmth. On the south side, at the river, sandpipers wing-dip in organised flocks. Occasionally I pass dog walkers and strolling couples, all of them offering a hello, or a nod of the head, which I acknowledge with a wan smile.

Continuing my walk, I turn north and east in a full square until I'm back at the gardens and the circle of benches surrounding the derelict fountain.

When I was a child, the fountain was the centrepiece of the park. The spume of water spurted high overhead, spraying showers of crystal droplets. How I loved to paddle in its maze of sun-rippled channels.

Once, I filled a bucket with cool water and chucked it over Mum's bare feet. Somewhere in the house there's a black and white photo of her in that fitted cotton dress, sitting beside the picnic basket, legs stuck out, anticipating the hit, looking like a young Bette Davis - plain but striking. I remember the dress was cream with a dark ivy pattern which, when she twirled, flared circles of windswept leaves.

That was when I could have told Mum anything. She always had a hug and a wise word. But now her face is naked — suspicion, surprise, and confusion plain to see. That independent woman who always had my back. How I need her now.

I choose a bench that's undecorated with white splats. A floral tribute lies limp on the arm of another across the way, every bloom a grieving head. Each bench has a brass plaque. When Mum passes maybe the family could donate a bench in her memory.

Molly McPhail loved these gardens

Sitting in the sun, I watch dogs zigzag, trot, then flop down panting on their bellies. Oh, for some of their energy. Stretching my legs, my knee joints crack. Avoiding the eyes of walkers passing by, I stare at my split nails, the dry crepe skin on my hands and wrists, and scratch a patch of eczema until blood pearls and streaks.

A boy appears at my left, dips his head to my level and grins, apparently unaware of personal space. His eyes shine midnight blue. He twists his face closer, mouth open, as if examining some specimen. My spine digs into the bench. The boy starts to hum, a half-sung chant. I scan the park for some attendant, parent, carer.

A woman hurries to the bench. "Sorry, sorry." She's smiling cheerily. "Turn my back and he's off." She tugs the boy by the arm. "Aiden, leave the nice lady be."

"Aiden," I repeat and bite back the word. Too late, it's taken as encouragement.

He laughs. The woman beams. Must be his gran. Grey, wiry, short hair and deep lines from eyes to chin. Dressed in smart grey trousers and white blouse.

"That's my boy." She ruffles his thatch of black hair; he rests his temple on her arm.

"Your grandson?" Though I can't see any resemblance.

"You're my boy aren't you, Aide?"

He grins with pleasure, leans into her.

They seem content to crowd my space. An almost empty park and I can neither rise nor move sideways.

"Lovely day," she says.

The boy thumps down, puts an arm around my neck, his thighs pushing into mine. Every nerve ending screams. I can't tolerate such closeness these days, but my sense of propriety forces me to smile.

"Lovely day," she says again.

She sits next to Aiden, pulls him to her and, as he's being inched away, I let out an audible breath.

The woman says, "Sorry, he's just very affectionate. Not always a good thing. Not everyone likes that . . . understands."

"It's fine, really. He's a . . . happy child. Very . . . active."

Aiden bounces up and jumps away after a Scots terrier who's more than willing to duck and dive with him. The woman perches at the edge of the bench, smiling fondly, a pink glow on her cheeks.

"My foster son," she offers.

"Oh."

The smile slips. "Don't say I'm marvellous, that you couldn't do it."

I bite back the words. "No, no, not at all . . ."

"People say I must have a heart of gold, as if he's an affliction. Makes me mad."

Aiden's on the ground, rolling with the dog. The owner's standing nearby, looking around quizzically.

The woman ignores the man's discomfort. "You have kids?" she says.

"Two, grown up, away at university."

"You're from around here?"

"Yes, local." I don't want this interest. I try to distract her. "I love this park."

"Underused. Good for us, eh?" She turns and looks at me with clear, green eyes winged with a network of lines.

I can't help but smile.

Aiden darts back, sits between us, and strokes my sleeve, head twisted up to my face. He smells of grass and soil, his shirt smeared green.

"Aiden. Sit here." She pats the bench close to her.

He shifts over to her side, and wraps himself around her, still staring at me.

"He's taken to you," she says.

"Sad," he blurts out, his eyes misting.

"Oh," we say in unison.

She inclines her head towards me in a question.

Flustered, I pick on the problem that's closest to the surface. "I was just sitting here thinking about getting a bench when my mum passes away."

"Oh, I am sorry. She's very ill?"

"Well, not terminal, no . . . just dementia."

"Just dementia . . ." She raises her eyes to the sky, shakes her head. "Awful thing. Personality transplant, eh?"

"That's it exactly."

"My mother went the same way. Oh, they didn't call it dementia or Alzheimer's then. It was just seen as old age, but it was awful." She shivers. "Thought we were stealing her money."

I try to dislodge the images. Mum sitting on the couch like a rag doll, propped up, her head lolling; trotting every half hour to the toilet, clop, clop, clop in her outdoor shoes; asking permission to go into her own kitchen; exclaiming that she's terrified, there's a strange man in the house; hiding her hearing aid. The lost rings, watch, cash. Mum folding her paper hankies, placing them in her glasses case, a perfect row of little squares.

"Mine too - she said that this afternoon. Wouldn't eat

lunch. Very agitated, watching me like I was a stranger. Accused me of stealing her purse."

It feels disloyal to speak of her like this. I change the subject. "How long have you had Aiden?"

"Since he was two, that's ten years. I'm Lily, by the way."

"Gillian."

The trees at the far end of the park move in the breeze. Clumped close together they form a mobile pattern of wood, leaf and sky that begins to fuse and melt.

I attempt a bit of humour. "Do you foster old people too?"

"Couldn't handle that." She laughs.

"But . . ." I nod at Aiden.

"That's a completely different kettle of fish."

"Fish, fish fish . . ." he chants, springing up. He swims over to the next bench, copying the breaststroke, and sinks down onto his belly, legs akimbo, pushing away imaginary water.

I venture, "Don't say you couldn't do what I'm doing." We both smile. Aiden floats up and whoops.

"I get a lot of support with Aiden, you know. There's a team of us and he has day care and I have respite. His mother helps too."

"Oh . . . that's nice."

We sit in silence for a moment. I break it. "I've thought of a care home for Mum, but I can't do it."

"No?"

"Well, it's like I'd be abandoning her." I stare at the distant trees, their swaying sun-dappled tapestry.

"What support does she have?"

"She has Home Care. And me, my husband, my brother, and a good friend."

"Get on to the GP. Make a fuss if you have to. Home Care's very good, takes the pressure off. But comes a time . . . there's drugs now too. To help the paranoia, agitation . . . all that."

"She's on those."

"Get stronger ones." Her eyes narrow. "You're awful peaky looking, dearie." She takes a breath. "It's not my place, but think about what your mum, if she were herself, would advise you."

I know the answer to that. The woman who always had my back.

Aiden's tugging Lily's blouse and she's on her feet. "Short attention span," she says. "Bye, lovey."

They fade away into the treeline.

Trespass
By Mike Watson

The room is silent except for the clock on the mantelpiece and the purring of the gas fire in the hearth.

"What was that noise?" asks Edith suddenly, glancing anxiously at Charles. Her question interrupts their peace and startles him. She puts her sewing down; he closes his book.

"Are you expecting someone?"

"Like who?"

"Well . . . I don't know . . . I just wondered."

"There it is again. Talking and laughing. Can you hear it? There are people in the garden."

Charles frowns. He has heard nothing but that isn't unusual. Edith has often joked about his 'selective hearing'. Yet one more malfunction in his old body. He is about to speak when Edith puts a finger to her lips and cocks her head to one side, like a bird.

"Shh! Did you hear it that time?"

Charles nods slowly. He eases himself up from the armchair,

stands a moment to correct his balance and walks over to the window. Drawing the curtains slightly, he peers outside.

A car passes by and in the headlights he spots shadows, like black rags, next to the front door. Forcing himself to focus, he sees there are two figures huddled together on the doorstep.

He taps on the window, making the figures jump. They glance in his direction then run down the short path, slam the metal gate and dash off. They disappear behind a long, dark bunch of bushes across the road.

"It's just kids," he says. "Well, teenagers more like. Two of them. They were on the doorstep. No idea what they were up to, but they've run across the road, behind the bushes."

"But what were they doing in our garden? Standing on our doorstep?"

Charles shrugs and closes the curtains. "I'm going outside," he says. "I'm going to see what they've been up to."

"But they've gone now, Charles. Don't bother."

"I just want to see. It's our house. Our front door. And . . . we've got every right to have a peaceful evening without being disturbed by a . . . by a couple of bloody kids!"

Edith follows him and watches as he unlocks the door. The chill of night air brushes her face and she hugs herself. Charles looks round the garden, unsure of what he's looking for. Mess? Signs of disturbance? He walks down the path, closes the gate, and looks up and down the street. Nothing.

It is only when he returns to the house that he notices a

scrap of paper attached to the door frame. He pulls the paper free and examines it.

"What's that, Charles? Is it a note or something? What does it say?"

Charles is reluctant to show Edith the paper but eventually he does. There is a crude drawing of a penis and four scribbled words:

PISS OF OLD BUGGERS

Her stomach clenches as if a punch has been thrown and she feels sick.

"They can't even get the insult right," he mutters.

Suddenly, there is a yell from the other side of the street and two teenage boys emerge from behind the bushes. They are laughing and shouting and making gestures with their hands and fingers. Then in one rapid movement, they both jerk down their jeans and expose their bottoms, wiggling them side to side.

When the grotesque performance is finished, they run off, hooting with laughter and eventually disappear down an alley.

The door is now locked and bolted again but their house does not feel the same. For the moment, Edith and Charles do not want to return to the front room. It is too close to the street and the vanished teenagers. Too close to the trespass of their home. Too close to the mean and undeserved insult. They retreat to the rear of the house, to the kitchen.

Edith's face is pale and drawn. She is tearful and with a

trembling hand, she stirs a pot of tea over and over and over again. Charles sits open-mouthed at the small wooden table and taps a finger against the top, as if sending for help using Morse code.

Neither Edith nor Charles can recall the happy years spent together, or the faces of their children and grandchildren. In their minds they replay, like a continuous loop, the intrusive events that have just soured their lives and left them staring at the days ahead.

Feeling Our Way Back
By Marion Horton

To begin with, it was a relief just to be out of the sun. And any relief was welcome.

"Up there," you had pointed. Your skinny arm lost in the baggy t-shirt you insisted on wearing.

The air had been a shimmer of jelly above the tarmac where the road became a winding path of small rocks. A splintered wooden sign pointed to a cliff face. We had found them, the caves you were so keen to explore. You had scrambled on ahead, stones skittering under your sandals.

Once inside the cave, I could hear your excited voice, echoing ahead of me, fading. You'd snatched a torch from me, light juddering off the rocky walls, and rushed on. I'd tried to tell you to be careful, slow down, but then I had found myself smiling at your enthusiasm, rare these days.

I would happily have just sat on the cool rock floor, taken a swig of water, and enjoyed the view. But maternal guilt had tugged me to go further in, leaving an oval of bright

Mediterranean light behind me.

The cave narrowed a few yards in and lowered. As I bent down, a tingle of panic edged over me. I called out to you, but you either didn't hear or you just didn't want to. Then, thankfully, the space opened up and there I was, in a huge, wide cavern.

Walls glistened in my torchlight, and green strands of vegetation hung in shaggy clumps. And far up I could see a circle of sky, casting a faint cone of light down into the cavern.

I waved my torch around, my panic evaporating, and some markings caught my eye. A fan of faded hand shapes was spread across the lower part of the wall, where the rock was flatter. I walked over and put my hand up to one of the outlines, and it fitted perfectly within. My hand tingled as it pressed against the rock, prickles pulsing in my fingers.

Then the torch began flickering. I slapped it, but it was dead, and when I searched in my pockets for my phone all I found was a cheap charm you had insisted I buy at a local market. Yet a light continued to flicker from behind me. I heard a splitting sound, like the crack of a thin bone breaking, and as I turned around red sparks jumped from a small fire burning on the ground, several yards into the cavern.

It was then I saw her. Crouched down, spitting onto a heap of ash, making some sort of dark paste. A re-enactment, no doubt, for tourists. I had noticed no activity when I entered the cavern, but then lately I had been so pre-occupied with your problems, barely sleeping, that perhaps it was no surprise.

I watched silently. The woman, for surely it was a woman, wore a wrap of fur, her hair was wild, her feet bare. She held a hand against the wall next to her and daubed the dark paste around her fingers. As she stepped back to view the shape that she had left on the rock she let out a primal call – of recognition, of delight? I couldn't say. I felt I had witnessed something astonishing – staged, but memorable nevertheless.

Then you called out. Your voice distressed, muffled from a darkness beyond the cavern. I stumbled towards the sound, my eyes fixing on your distant torchlight.

You had tripped. Your face wet with pain and disappointment. You had placed such importance on seeing these caves – I had no idea why – and now your exploration was to end with a twisted ankle. You tried to bat me away as I reached to wipe your tears and my fingers left an ashy streak on your cheeks.

"Lean on me. Come and see this." I hauled you up, though you resisted, and half-dragged you back to the cavern.

But it was empty. There was no sign of the cave woman or the fire. Just us, and the cone of light from the skyhole metres above. You shook your head in disbelief. What stories would I make up next? You weren't a child any more! I kept my thoughts to myself. So we stood there, not speaking.

You swung your torch around, as if to emphasise that we were alone, and the beam fell onto the fan of faded hand shapes on the wall. You hobbled over and put your own childlike hand against one of the smaller shapes, resting it within the faded outline. Your thin frame shivered and then you turned around and gave a quiet gasp. You told me to look, Mum, look there! You could see a girl, a bit like you, and an older woman, and a fire. They were making handprints together. Couldn't I hear them laughing? You pointed at the spot, but what I saw was the look of wonder on your stained face.

The images dwindled and disappeared from your sight, although you said later you could still hear their strange language filling the air as we had remained transfixed, caught in something we didn't understand, nor need to. And when eventually we began to make our slow way out of the caves, we moved carefully and quietly, keeping the memory gently wrapped within us so that we would not lose it. Not wanting to speak it out loud.

As we stood by the cave entrance, assessing the steep track back to the car, I reached into my pocket for tissues to wipe away the dirt from your cheeks. The charm came out with the tissues. You took it and let it swing from your fingers. It was a small fragment of rock in the shape of a hand. And as I dabbed at your face with a tissue, you reached out your arms and hugged me tightly.

A Burglar's Recital
and the Profit of Eleven Burglaries
By Diane Milhan

April 12 to May 1, 1919 – Rochester, New York

Robert LeCompte: Elmer pulled off that job hisself. Got pinched by hisself. He had my gun. I have told you everything else. I have made a clean breast of things. I was not there.

A gold watch worth 25 dollars

The first burglary on April 12 was in the home of Arthur Nash, a real estate agent, who had arrived from Russia in 1894 and lived with wife and daughter.

Goose Egg

The second burglary on this same night was at 431 Grand Avenue, nine houses west. This was the home of E Bosse, a self-employed tailor. Both of his wife's parents were born in Germany and the couple had a 17-year-old daughter named Marion, who attended the University of Rochester. All the furniture was draped with fabric, but no garments the boys thought worth the exercise of stealing.

A package of Murad Turkish cigarettes and a Red Dot cigar tin with five moldy cigars worth 15 dollars

The final break-in of the night was at 425 Parsells Avenue, north on Denver and west on Parcells, just past the house that Elmer lived in with his sister and brother and grandmother. Louis E Heindl, a native Rochestarian whose parents were born in Bavaria, resided in his in-laws' home with his wife and daughter, 24-year-old Helen.

A soprano ukulele worth three dollars

The next night at the home of Fred Deininger at 274 Barrington Street. Deininger's parents and his wife's parents were born in Germany. Deininger had recently sold his bake shop to a larger company. The family had a 19-year-old daughter, Kathryn Louise.

***

Pattern showing here? Head of household speaks with an accent that could be taken as German and the presence of a younger woman that could be imagined as overture. This at a time after the war when German-American businesses and homes were still vandalized.

The boys, Elmer Hyatt and Robert LeCompte, had both been members of the New York National Guard, but were never called to France. A singular disappointment for Elmer. Burglary of these four households was an adventure to crow about, still pursuing a defeated imagined enemy and sharing heated thoughts of flesh. What strange combination of hate to the Huns and hope for the hump.

The burglaries had actually started earlier in the afternoon of April 12 when the two boys found a way into No 33 School on Grand Avenue and rummaged classrooms for trophies.

Nothing worth carrying off

No 33 School on Grand Avenue. No objects enticing enough for a 16 and a 17-year-old to haul off. When the evening was so young, why carry around stuff you do not want anyway? However, reprisal for no scorable booty was imposed by writing profanity on chalkboards and by scratching onto a small tablet the words SOME CHICKEN.

Robert LeCompte: "I am telling you, Captain. Elmer thought he was a cock-a-doodle rooster. In a henhouse school. 'Some chicken' my ass. Elmer thinks he is so game with the girls. Always on the make. I said, 'What are you smiling about so big' and he squawked that he could hardly guess what the girl who picked up the tablet would feel. That was when I whipped the silly look of his face with my fist and knocked him a few times in the noodle as if that could wake him up to think like me. Nitwitted little wanker. Anyways, he wanted to fly out of there."

The burglars take off Easter Week and go to the Saturday Victory Loan Parade down Mainstreet, celebrating the National

Guard soldiers who are still returning home from France. Some of these celebrated soldiers were their friends from the 3rd Guard at the Armory.

Robert LeCompte: "Elmer was dying to see our old guys from the Armory, the ones coming back from France. There would be whippet tanks, fully equipped. A battlefield prize of war. And a German tank captured by the 27th Division. But his brother was not in the parade. He stayed in France, holding down the German population. The parade made Elmer screech at me. Did I see this and did I see that. He asked me about the revolver that I said I had. I told him that I made the story up. It was not true. I did have a gun. I sang just to piss him:

They breached the line in a Tiger tank,
One to drive and two to wank,
Hinky Dinky parlez vous."

Nothin' but the smell of lavender on their shoes

Burglars passed on Carpo-Naptha soap at the first home and on Shinon Silver Polish jar at the second. Two homes with women living alone. Tuesday, after Easter, into the home of young widow Clara Howard at 242 Brunswick Street. Saturday night on April 26 at the home of Elizabeth Moore at 179 Grand. Just lady stuff.

Robert LeCompte: "Elmer was really pissed that we had not got any goods that evening so we hauled down to the railroad yard at Havens. I knew that the yegg had pilfered my shooter. Elmer thought that I did not know, but how could I not miss the revolver. Was I surprised when he whipped out my revolver and held it to the belly of a conductor, working alone in the yards. The man started to push back against Elmer, but Elmer was determined to hold onto the man to pinch his receipts from the day. When the conductor broke free and backed away, Elmer only aimed the gun at the man's feet. The punk stood there and watched the man climb the fence and drop to the other side."

Jack Squat

The first two houses on Tuesday evening, April 29, were entered but nothing was taken. The Shumway house at 100 Brunswick followed by a long walk west to Campbell home at 245 Glasser Street. The burglars headed west again and crossed the Genesee River walking along the mule pathway of the Erie Canal aqueduct.

One man's shirt size 17, one necklace with pearls, and a black cowhide traveling bag worth 50 dollars

Down Shumway to Canterbury on the same night to the home of Dr Edwin Ingersoll, an ear, nose and throat physician who had spent seven months treating mustard gas exposed soldiers in France. A 17-year-old servant girl named Elenor lived in the house.

The chunky skeleton key that opened the front door

Two nights later, Thursday, 1 May, 709 Garson Avenue was entered with a key, but nothing was stolen. Key later found on front porch. James McNany was foreman at Morgan Machine on University Avenue.

Pair of opera glasses and a gold ring worth 15 dollars
Same night, next door at 715 Garson, home of William Milander, a locomotive engineer. Both of his parents were German born. Milander later tells the police that the burglars missed 600 dollars in bills and 400 dollars in Liberty Bonds in a drawer that was not opened. What might have been different if the burglars had scored that money?

Robert LeCompte: "Elmer would still not shut up about the army tank from the parade. He thinks about guns and war and getting to the army rumpus in France to fight Jerry like his brother, but that will never happen. He could not even make it in the Guard because of his eyes. He griped my ass off so bad that he would not give me the gun back and I told him if he was so cocksure to go do the job hisself tonight. He crowed that he would go out without me. And me stoney broke, I could really use some stuff to pawn. By hisself and without me to guide him, it means that he will stay up where we have already been hitting the same area. I told him the idea was bad and he would get copped. But besides that, I was going early to see Louise, who told me that she had surprises for me. I told him I would meet him later but I was not going to promise to show up."

Four cigars, two oranges, and a can of Borden's evaporated milk. One dead policeman with a bullet to the heart. One bullet to the lower chest of Elmer

Friday, May 2, at 290 Garson Avenue, home of the Lovetts. Here lives a 20-year-old daughter.

Robert LeCompte: "No, sir, I was not there, I was not anywhere near where that shooting went down. I was away with my girl who spends sweet money on me. Elmer went to that house alone. I was with him the night before but not on that night. I have told you everything I know about that night because I was not there."

Pterippus
By Rob Nisbet

I suppose we must have been asleep, the young Nadia and me. Gradually we become conscious until we think we are awake, but we don't open our eyes – *that* is too much effort.

We are lulled by suffocating warmth, too tired to move, too tired to wonder where we are. Even our breathing: softly in, softly out, is an effort; we just want to lie here, undisturbed, never get up.

We assume, without the need to think, that we are in our bedroom, the young Nadia and me. But there are other people here too. They talk in whispers as if keeping secrets from us. I don't recognise their voices and I am far too weary to work out what they are saying.

After a while we manage to open our eyes. There are the shapes of two people looming over us. A bedside light glimmers, but the main light is off. It is a strain to see them. They are as shadowy and indistinct as their whispers. The curtains are drawn to preserve a reverent gloom; we are not sure that it is night outside.

"Back with us, Mum?" A young man leans into the light. His teeth smile at us, but not his eyes. "The doctor says you should be . . . " he pauses, still smiling, blinks those sad eyes, "comfortable."

Well, we're not comfortable. My breathing is stifled; the room is stuffy and dark. And I am so very tired. I want this man to pull back the curtains, open the window, let in some air. Who are these people? The young Nadia has a better memory than I do, but they are strangers to her too, even the one who calls us Mum. We follow them with our eyes. We do not trust them and say nothing.

With his great wings spread, a clown flies down through the ceiling, unnoticed by the two intruders.

***

We see the clown, the old Nadia and me. The old Nadia is unphased by his arrival. Her mind no longer questions, merely observes, with a confused acceptance. But for me there is a stirring of recollection. The clown has wild orange hair, a bulbous red nose, and an outlandish painted grin: a ridiculous but genuine smile that shines from his eyes. His great white wings fold into place at his back, and his too-baggy trousers wobble on their braces as he crosses to the window. He pulls back the curtains. He opens the window to the welcome, cool scent of the fields. It is night, after all.

And we are outside. The old Nadia is slow and fragile,

but she draws a little strength from me. I help her shuffle up the slope and we disappear quietly into the night before the strangers in our room notice.

The track is dark and pitted, but at each corner a clown flutters down, wings glowing, to guide us. From deep within her wrinkles, the old Nadia blinks at the clowns with innocent wonder. But I feel the old memories stir within her, and for once we both know where we are going: The Top Field, at the crest of the hill, where Domino will be waiting for us.

Margaret and Charlotte are there too, of course. Someone had told the old Nadia that they'd died, years ago, Domino too. I sympathise. I don't want to become the old Nadia. My memory is stronger. I am Nadia at nineteen; Margaret and Charlotte are in their early twenties. We are inseparable. We call Domino, the old Nadia and me, our voice almost lost in the vast night. But she hears us and trots over the crest, a black shadow against the slightly brighter sky flecked with stars. We feed her soft lips a carrot from our pocket.

We lead her to the circle of hay bales. Charlotte hauls one bale aside and we guide Domino into our home-made circus ring. The old Nadia hasn't remembered Domino for years, and I feel her delight. I guide her hands and we pat her dark flanks, spotted with white as if draped in constellations. Margaret points to the sky, tracing a line from the Plough to find the North Star: the Pole Star. From our point of view, she says, the whole universe revolves around this point. The old Nadia and me aren't really interested; we feed Domino another carrot. Charlotte is more enthusiastic, "Where's Pegasus?" she asks.

And Margaret swings round to point at a square of stars. "A pterippus," she says. "A winged horse." Charlotte and I roll our eyes; only Margaret would know a word like that.

We clamber onto a bale, the old Nadia and me, while Margaret and Charlotte watch by starlight. Then we are up and onto Domino's back. No saddle. We trot around the circle, bouncing into Domino's step. The old Nadia clings nervously in the darkness, but I remind her how to ride, relax her hands and we pick up speed.

Charlotte whoops and sings, her blonde curls bobbing in the breeze. She is always the audience, applauding as we circle faster and faster. Margaret is the Ringmaster. She stands dark and serious in the centre, waving a stick, conducting the show.

The old Nadia delights in the night-time ride. She depends on me; I feel her cling to my memories; firmer than the fleeting blur I see through her eyes. We remember our circus plans, how we dreamt of performing in a costume of star-spangles, the crowd would cheer and gasp as we and Domino juggled, balanced on barrels and leapt through hoops of fire.

We slow Domino to a trot, carefully draw up our legs to kneel on her back and circle our hay-bale ring a few times. Then we stand, arms stretched wide for balance. The audience roars like a thousand lions. We raise one leg behind us, lean into Domino's rhythm for a whole circuit. The old Nadia's memories can't see the fall coming. The ground is uneven and hard. We tumble like an acrobat.

The pain in our arm is sharp. We know it is broken. The audience shrieks its dismay. We end up in hospital, a heavy plaster cast, no riding for at least two months.

***

My dreams summersault around that point. I feel my life pivot, and a skein of memory drifts from the young Nadia, through the intervening years, till it brushes me, light as a cobweb. No more tricks on Domino, though she remained our closest companion. Our fantasy of circus life shifts to a more mundane performance. We grow, we work, we marry, we have a child, we age, we decline. Domino lives another 20 years, Margaret and Charlotte 20 more. And we open our eyes in our stuffy bedroom to a doctor, and our son with that unhappy smile.

We try to smile back, the young Nadia and me. But even that is too much for us. The men by our bed become strangers again, and our twist of memory unravels like our ridiculous, impractical circus dreams.

The clown by the window catches our eyes, tugs back the curtains. And we long for the cool darkness; to be accepted in the embrace of night.

And we are back in the Big Top Field. Our costume glitters like the stars. The folded sky is draped over the circus ring, anchored in place to a pole through the Earth. Pegasus shines spotlights onto us as we stand on Domino's back, arms stretched wide for balance. The audience roars above the music, and we recognise them, every one: Margaret, Charlotte, our husband, our son. And, somewhere in my past, the young Nadia settles back where she belongs. A thousand voices cheer for us. We raise one leg behind us, lean forward into Domino's rhythm for a whole circuit. Domino's progress is smooth, unfolding wings that we hadn't noticed before. The clowns flutter up around us, and we sparkle into the starry sky.

On the Shoreline
By David Miller

The track leading to the beach is narrow and dusty; full of ruts and bumps.

The jeep jumps and sways as we jolt our way along. The wheels kick up clouds of fine sand.

I don't meet your glances on the way down, pretending I need full concentration on driving. Nor do we talk; in silence we pass ragged gorse-bushes; stunted pine trees. A few of these bear a crop of thin cones, others are bare, even their needles have turned brown.

The beach is deserted at this hour, the few holiday-makers who find this isolated sport long departed. All signs that there were ever any other visitors now covered by the drifting sands.

We stand; facing each other, but in silence.

Too full of emotions to speak.

Shall I ask you again to change your mind?

I know you won't.

I can't, you'll say again. I can't live in this world.

It's your world, not mine. And I must leave it.

So I don't argue now. Nothing further to say.

No points not made, no arrows of logic not fired.

But my logic makes no impression on your logic.

It cannot, and I do know that. I do know that.

A sharp wind begins, I shiver.

I look out over the sea, silent and silver. To me, coldly grey, empty, unwelcoming.

Neither haven nor safe harbour.

To you?

You begin to undress: provocatively, I say.

You say not.

Soon you are naked.

Memories make a tumult in my mind, but you look eagerly towards the ocean.

Eagerly towards the end. For one of us.

Again, neither of us speaks. We stand, we stand.

At length you say, Now.

I nod. Not moving.

You smile for the first time.

Carry me. Carry me as you did when first we met.

Just until . . . until . . .

Ah, when first we met.

And a hundred memories return, a thousand.

Must this really be?

But I lift you, and walk across the damp sand towards the

rippling waves. Towards the end.

The salt water reaches my knees, my waist, my chest.

Your legs begin to tremble at the water's touch, it is the change.

A last kiss, and then I let you go.

I let you go, and with a flip of your strong, green tail you are gone.

Back to your world.

And I return to mine.

Alone.

Alone.

Alone.

Charlotte
By Graham Crisp

Charlotte arrived a few days after I regained consciousness. She politely introduced herself and remained quietly with me as I began to gain strength.

I could only recall fragments of the fire that had so rapidly and ferociously ripped through the upstairs of my home. I had just left the bathroom when I was engulfed in thick grey smoke that tore through my body. I remember the ambulance and the green-uniformed paramedics covering part of my face and the upper area of my left arm with something that felt like clingfilm. Then nothing – until Charlotte gently called my name, and we were together.

I suppose I should have asked her why she had chosen me. I mean, there were two other girls on either side of me and another three opposite, but Charlotte had singled me out and at first I was grateful for her company.

Charlotte always stepped away when I was being examined. It seemed the right thing for her to do. She strongly suggested that we should keep our relationship just between the two of us and so I abided by her wishes.

It was on a Wednesday, on a wonderful bright sunny afternoon, that my bandages were removed. I could sense a high level of anticipation, as my consultant and a nurse approached me and drew the curtains tightly around my bed. I knew Charlotte was there somewhere. I could sense her presence.

The dressings fell away easily, and for the first time in several months, the left side of my face and shoulder were exposed to the world. Although the warm sun shone through an opened window, my face, shoulder and arm were frozen. It was as if they were indifferent to the summer sun. A dull ache pressed down on my newly exposed skin. The consultant examined me, nodding slowly. I heard him prescribe some painkillers and something unpronounceable. The nurse nodded and slipped through the curtains.

My consultant's name was Mr Balay. Every time I heard his name being called, I had cheeky visions of him dressed in skinny tights as he danced across the ward, pirouetting and leaping past the nurse station and onto his next patient, immediately followed by his junior doctor clad in a starched white tutu tip-toeing elegantly behind him.

The vision of Mr Balay's Swan Lake soon deserted as I observed a deep frown that began to form across his brow. He calmly explained that I was *heavily scarred* but the scars would *thin* out over time, and there was the option of some *surgery* at a later date. His voice lowered to just above a whisper: I should *prepare myself* before I took up his offer of a mirror.

Mr Balay gave me a thin smile and backed away. I was momentarily alone. The large hand mirror lay alongside me.

Then Charlotte was there.

I lifted the mirror to my face, and immediately dropped it back.

The word hideous sprang into my mind.

Charlotte was kind. She reassured me that I was far from hideous and that my hair, when fully grown back, would cover a large part of my face. And yes, I might feel that off-the-shoulder dresses would make me feel a little conspicuous, but that wasn't the end of my world. Charlotte's soothing reassurances calmed me. She made me feel consoled and comforted.

***

A few weeks later, fully dressed in a high-necked patterned dress, sporting puff sleeves and with heavy concealer liberally applied to the left side of my face, I prepared to leave the safe confines of the ward. The nurses and staff had lined up like a guard of honour; they each touched my hands and bade me good wishes as I headed towards the exit. Charlotte followed me out. I could hear her encouraging and supportive words.

Now I had Charlotte I felt I was ready to regain my place in the world.

My confidence grew, and as my sixteenth birthday approached, I decided that I would celebrate it with a big party.

Strangely, Charlotte wasn't very impressed with my plans. She tried to get me to change my mind, or at least scale things back.

Normally I would acquiesce to Charlotte but this time, I ignored her. No matter how much she nagged me, I planned my party and invited just about everyone I knew.

I danced with a well fit guy called Charlie. I recall we briefly kissed. As he left, we made arrangements to meet again. I felt whole now, the scars may still be visible on the outside, but inside I was at peace.

As the last guests left, I sat down at the bottom of the stairs and contemplated. The party had been perfect. Okay, I did notice on occasions that some of the invitees surreptitiously pointed at me, and whispered behind cupped hands, but I was now used to this and I certainly wasn't going to let it spoil my fun. And the best bit? My future date with Charlie. Was he going to be my first boyfriend?

I had enjoyed myself so much that it was only later that I realised that Charlotte hadn't been anywhere near me for the whole evening. I just shrugged, stood up, and climbed the stairs.

However, Charlotte returned when I entered my bedroom. I remember immediately sensing a foreboding atmosphere. Charlotte was angry. She positively growled. She was hard and menacing. She said that the whole evening had been a complete disaster. That Charlie was only after one thing, and that the girls had sniped about my clothes and makeup behind my back.

Charlotte's taunts and torments continued relentlessly. Her previous gentle and supportive nature had been replaced by cruel threats, insults, and vile abuse. I pleaded with her to stop, but this just made her worse.

Things got so desperate that after another evening of vilifications from Charlotte, I found myself locked in the bathroom clutching a full bottle of sleeping pills. I could feel Charlotte's menacing encouragement, goading me to swallow. I gathered myself and dropped the bottle. The pills spilled out across the floor.

This was the final straw. I faced down Charlotte. I forcibly told her that I no longer needed her, or wanted her, and that she should go. Immediately. I pushed her away.

Then I felt a sharp stabbing pain in my left shoulder.

But the insults stopped.

Charlotte had gone.

Recalling that decisive moment, I closed my eyes and ran my finger down the scars on the side of my face.

***

About two months after Charlotte's disappearance, on a wonderful sunny afternoon, I was sitting with Charlie on a park bench nibbling an orange ice lolly, when I heard a girl's voice. I turned around. From the back I guessed that she was around fifteen or sixteen. She seemed to be alone and it looked like she was talking to herself.

Thinking that she might be in some distress, I strained my

ears to hear her words.

My blood ran cold.

Although her voice was hushed, I could clearly make out what she was saying.

"Look Charlotte, I can go out with whoever I like! You can't stop me! And don't call him that. Steve is a nice guy, he wouldn't do anything like that. I don't know what's come over you, you were, you know, like, so kind to me in hospital – now you're being really horrible! Just leave me alone!"

I tugged at Charlie's arm and quickly dragged him away.

Clearance
By Philippa Howell

Angie found the letter on the third day. It was in Mum's bedside cabinet, tucked behind a perished rubber douche and a packet of tissues covered in small pink roses. Like everything else in the house, the letter was a little damp. It was addressed to Mum, but the postmark was long gone. Angie studied the unfamiliar handwriting then popped the letter in the pocket of her overall. She must get on. The old place was almost empty.

It dawned on Angie that it would always be 'The Old Place' now, no longer home. An unremarkable three-storey house on a main road. Somewhere and nowhere.

Angie picked up a framed photo lying on the windowsill. There was Mum in her wedding dress, and Dad as proud as a pigeon, his arm around Mum's tiny waist. Ray and Jean. Looking at them, Angie wondered again why they had waited fifteen years to have her. Perhaps there were 'difficulties' in that department, but she hadn't liked to ask. She studied their faces and tried to remember at what point her parents had stopped being young and started to get old. There was no change from day to day but go back sixty-five years to this photo. *My God, what a difference.*

She was 40 when she had finally moved into her own place. Mum and Dad gave her the deposit so there were no more excuses. After she left, she took to calling in on them after work. But they took to being out around that time.

Angie worked in credit control, and was known to be a bit of a rottweiler when it came to chasing debtors. She would regale Mum and Dad with stories of her daily battles and triumphs. They listened but never seemed proud, which made her wonder if she had left something out.

On the last Sunday of every month Mum and Dad came to her place for dinner. Angie spent the week planning the menu. She would shop at the market on the Saturday morning. In the evening she'd write out the menu, date it, cover it in sticky-back plastic and prop it up against the condiments on the kitchen table. After the meal, when Mum and Dad went home, she would slide the menu into a folder labelled *Dinners for Mum and Dad*. At the last count she had 143 menus. She made plain food for them, nothing fancy like tagine or chocolate fondants; those were for her to eat alone.

Angie realised she was still staring at her parents' wedding photo. She put it down, and turned back to the job in hand. There was a heap of handbags in the middle of the floor, and she began emptying them into a bin bag, scattering safety pins, bus tickets, and coins. From a velvet evening bag, a golden lipstick case clattered on to the floor. Picking it up, she could just make out the label, *Crimson Kiss*. Mum had always looked so nice in that colour.

Looking out of the window on to the garden below. Angie could picture Dad in his old raincoat, pushing his wheelbarrow between the raised beds. His coat was still hanging on a peg by the back door. She knew that at some point, she would bury her face in it.

For years before the accident, Mum had pestered Dad to get a toilet put in downstairs, but it didn't happen. The squabble was never sorted, and they continued to tug themselves up the banisters to the first-floor toilet when they needed to go. They had taken to coming down on their bottoms, stair by stair for safety's sake, like little kids. Angie offered more than once to move back in to help them. "No," said Mum. "Then there would be three of us needing the toilet. How would that help?"

One Saturday morning, Mum lost her balance after using the toilet and toppled down all fifteen stairs, landing outside the lounge. How she didn't break her neck nobody knew. Dad phoned for an ambulance but did not phone Angie, who only found out from the neighbours when she called in after work. Mum was in hospital with seven broken ribs, a broken arm and concussion. She was on heavy-duty pain killers and lost her mind for a few days. Thought she was a ballerina.

Angie took time off work and drove Dad to the hospital as

often as he would let her. On other days he would get the bus, and she would drive there on her own to find him sitting by Mum's bed, mute and watchful.

One sunny September evening Mum's light suddenly faded, and Dad watched it go out. Angie had popped to the loo and missed it. She felt cheated, always left out of things, even this. Dad was shaking like a leaf, but he refused Angie's outstretched arms.

After the funeral he told her it was time he went into a care home, and they must sell their house to pay for it. "I could come back and look after you, Dad," she said. Perhaps he didn't hear. A place at The Glen soon became available and Dad's life shrank to four walls, as is the way of things. A relay team of staff sorted him out, and when she visited Angie felt in the way.

She set about selling the house, and to her dismay it went very quickly. She found John, the Man with a Van, on a card in a post office window. He reckoned it would take three full days to clear everything from the house as there was a lot of it, and he only had the one Bedford. "Sixty-five years of 'it'll come in handy' eh?" he joked. She didn't laugh.

First, John and his lad dismantled and took away all the big stuff – beds, wardrobes, sideboards. Then on day two they cleared the top floor which had served as a dumping ground. The rooms had never been slept in and were stacked to the ceiling with rolls of cracked lino, Christmas baubles, surplus ceramic tiles, mouldy orange window blinds, and up to 100 bars of soap, their scent long gone.

There was a vintage projector with 22 boxes of slides still waiting for their premiere, a steam-powered sheet press, Angie's blue trike, and an iron mangle. "Who'd carry a mangle up three flights!" John laughed as he wrestled it down again. He and his lad ran up and down the stairs like ants with crumbs, driving full loads away in the van every hour or so.

Now it was finally the end of the third day. The clearance was finished. Angie walked silently through her life from the top floor to the cellar, turning off the lights as she went. Alone in the kitchen, she reached into her pocket for the backdoor key, and her hand closed on the letter.

Dear Jean, it read. *It is very good of you and Ray to take Angie in, especially as I know you don't want children of your own . . .*

Angie stood and cried, her mouth gaping like one of the cupboards. Finally, she took off her overall, and left home for the last time, locking the door behind her. She got into her car and drove the half mile to her terrace house where John was waiting.

He wound down his window. "Everything I can't get in your house I've put under a tarpaulin in the back yard. What are you going to do with that mangle then!" He was still laughing.

Angie looked him straight in the eye. "Fuck. Off."

Three weeks later the police broke down the front door. They found a woman's body, the head wedged at a nasty angle between a metal bedframe and a fallen cupboard. In her right hand was a handwritten letter.

The body was dressed in an old gentleman's raincoat.

Biographies

Aftermath **Heather Alabaster**

My husband and I live in Durham. I wrote stories and poems from early school years, although working in libraries and publishing was all about facts, not fiction. Since my focus changed, opening lines and themes fill my head and my notebook. I love creating characters to bring them alive.

Brownie **Angela Aries**

After many years of teaching and co-authoring textbooks, Angela is delighted to have more time to devote to fiction. She is particularly interested in writing historical novels, and loves doing the necessary research. She has recently completed her Roman trilogy, and is actively seeking publication. In her spare time, Angela enjoys singing and gardening.

Merci **Susan Axbey**

Susan Axbey is the author of a number of educational books and also writes fiction. Her story *The Opening* was longlisted for the Bridport Prize. She is currently working on a collection of short stories and flash fiction. After many years of travelling, Susan now lives in London.

A Bad Hair Day **Susan R Barclay**

Originally from Atlanta, Georgia, Susan R Barclay is retired but still a writer, educator, and thinker who now lives in Alabama, where she makes poor attempts at witticism. She enjoys pulling from life experiences to write both fiction and non-fiction.

The Edge **Gillian Brown**

Gillian Brown started out as a travel writer but her heart now lies in fiction. Her travels and real life experiences bring inspiration. Short story competitions give her motivation. For the latter she has a mild – but enjoyable – addiction.

A Mother's Love **Sue Buckingham**

My husband and I live near Cardiff and I own a horse. Having spent all my working life as an accountant wrestling with numbers, now retired I am fulfilling my dreams by wrangling words into order instead, and have finally finished my first novel.

Returning the Call　　　　　　　　　　　　**Carolyn Carter**

I write in the early morning. Time slows for a fresh page in the notebook and words ink in wherever I want to be. I don't always start at the beginning. I live in Sussex, where the landscape is beautiful. Since stopping teaching, there's room for everything.

The H&M Community　　　　　　　　　　**Elizabeth Cathie**

Elizabeth is a writer of short stories and poems, living in Herefordshire. Her writing is inspired by overheard snippets of conversation, by the people and events of daily life, and by a long-held habit of people watching. Her debut book, *Stories of Life and Love,* is available from Amazon *https://amzn.eu/d/es81hFs*

Charlotte　　　　　　　　　　　　　　　　**Graham Crisp**

Twenty-five years ago, I escaped the hustle and bustle of the West Midlands and now reside in a small village in Cambridgeshire, accompanied by my wife and two cats. I write short stories on a variety of subjects, although, worryingly, the 'afterlife' seems to feature in many of my stories.

Perfect Rows of Little Squares **Maureen Cullen**

Maureen Cullen lives in Argyll and Bute. In 2015, she was awarded an MA in Creative Writing from Lancaster University. She has stories and poems published in a range of magazines. In 2021, Maureen was shortlisted for the V S Pritchett Short Story Prize. Find Maureen on X/Twitter @ *maureengcullen*

A Memory of Lavender **Patricia Feinberg Stoner**

Patricia Feinberg Stoner is an award-winning British writer, a former journalist, copywriter and publicist. She is the author of the Pays d'Oc series: *At Home in the Pays d'Oc, Tales from the Pays d'Oc* and *Murder in the Pays d'Oc*, and three books of comic verse, see X/Twitter *@pawprints66*

The Lodger **Lynne Hackles**

I have been writing all my life. Most of my stories are for women's magazines. You never know what will happen when you write. I didn't expect to become a novelist at my age but last year my debut novel, Gail Lockwood and Her Imaginary Agony Aunt, was published by Cahill Davis.

You Sent Me Flowers **David Higham**

David Higham lives in Portsmouth. He and his wife enjoy kayaking in Langstone Harbour and travelling. David's travel blog is at www.theancienttraveller.com. David had three careers. First he was a submariner in the Royal Navy, then a lawyer and finally a visiting professor. David took up writing, wondering how hard it could be? Answer: very.

Feeling Our Way Back **Marion Horton**

I love writing short fiction and poetry and am currently studying for an MA in creative writing – we are never too old to learn! I also enjoy a bracing hike over the Sussex Downs or Dorset hills whenever the weather allows.

Clearance **Philippa Howell**

Professional actress, ex-restaurateur, ex-theatrical agent, now doting Granny. I live in a cottage on the border between Sheffield and the Peak District, nine miles from Chatsworth, two from my grandson. I write, draw, walk the hills, cook for friends, see films, and spoil my two rescue cats, Luna and Minnie.

The Reception **Ian Inglis**

Ian Inglis was born in Stoke-on-Trent and now lives in Newcastle-upon-Tyne. His short fiction has appeared in numerous anthologies and literary magazines in the UK and US, and his debut collection of short stories *The Day Chuck Berry Died* was published by Bridge House in Autumn 2022. *http://ianinglis15.wixsite.com/home*

Cold Hands and Bananas **Gwenda Major**

Born in Newcastle, Gwenda now lives in the beautiful Lake District. She was a teacher of deaf children and later worked in further education. Her interests include genealogy, gardens and graveyards. Many of her short and flash stories have appeared in print and now her ambition is to have one of her novels published.

Playtime **Brian McDonald**

Since retirement I spend my time swimming, watching Manchester City and writing. Teddy Edwards really exists. He currently lives on top of the wardrobe in the spare bedroom. This story is for William who loves monsters.

Just Three Words **John Maskey**

John Maskey is a journalist by trade and has been writing fiction for about eight years. He has had short stories published in the US and Australia as well as in the UK. He lives in Newcastle with his family and spends too much of his time watching football.

A Burglar's Recital **Diane Milhan**

Diane Milhan is a practicing acupuncturist in Mount Airy, North Carolina. She is writing a nonfiction version of the short life of her grand uncle, who is featured in this piece. The boy was the youngest man to be executed in Sing Sing prison in 1919.

On the Shoreline **David Miller**

Born in London, parents moved to Suffolk in 1958 where I now live. Attended local schools – moved to Chile in 1971 to work for my uncle who had a business there. Returned to England when this didn't work out, and went into shipping. Now retired I enjoy folk and shanty singing, and writing the occasional short story.

Goodbye Benjamin **Chris Milner**

Chris from Hexham in Northumberland has enjoyed a varied career as postman, lathe operator, hop picker, materials researcher, nuclear engineer, software engineer, social entrepreneur, charity manager, company director and trustee, but now enjoys grand-parenting duties and occasional writing about what was and what might be, especially if it's for a competition.

Farewell **Rob Molan**

Rob is a former civil servant and lives in Edinburgh. He started writing short stories during lockdown and later attended two creative writing courses at Edinburgh University. He has had a number of short stories published to date. Rob is always looking for ways of improving his writing, through feedback on his stories and reading the literary giants.

Turning a Blind Eye **Margaret Morey**

I have lived in Northumberland for the last fifty years, and have to remind myself that I grew up on Teesside and studied in Manchester and Leeds, so am not a true native. I have travelled extensively, mostly in Europe, usually to places with a better climate, although I love the Hebrides despite the rain and midges.

Pterippus **Rob Nisbet**

Rob Nisbet has had around 100 stories printed in anthologies and magazines ranging from romance to horror. He also writes audio drama: he has adapted work by Philip K Dick for radio and has had several audio scripts produced by Big Finish/BBC for their *Doctor Who* range.

The House **Mark Pearce**

Mark was delighted when early retirement afforded him the opportunity to commit more time to writing. Since then he has had several short stories published and completed a novel for NaNoWriMo. He is a member of several writing groups all based within Shropshire. He plans to publish a crime novel in 2024.

Ms Molly Gets Herself Noticed **Maggie Sinclair**

Maggie Sinclair is a self-confessed writing addict. She discovered flash fiction in 2020 and has been writing tiny stories ever since. Maggie recently retired from a career in community education and now lives in Perthshire, Scotland with her endlessly patient husband, a badly-behaved tabby cat and a flock of chickens.

Mother's Wise Words **Nicola Spain**

Nicola Spain graduated in 2020 from Newcastle University with an MA in Creative Writing. She has had short stories published in a number of anthologies and been successful in various writing competitions. Having recently retired from her work as a solicitor, she is currently combining her legal knowledge and writing passion into a courtroom-based novel.

A Good Report **Graham Steed**

I am a 74 year old retired teacher of Mathematics. I published a novel, *The Young Robinson Crusoe,* on Amazon in 2014. I wrote a short story for the Saudi Historical Novel Society and won £1000! I'm writing my second novel, the *Story of Marg:* a crime writer investigates a death on the ghost train.

The Census Taker **Lou Storey**

Lou Storey is a visual artist and retired psychotherapist living in Savannah, Georgia, with Steve, his husband of thirty-five years. Lou's writings have appeared in *The New Yorker, New York Times Tiny Love Stories,* River Teeth's *Beautiful Things, Blue Mountain Literary Review, Multiplicity Magazine,* and *Beyond Queer Words Anthology.*

Betty's Boyfriend **Anne Thomson**

Anne Thomson lives in South Devon. She has been shortlisted in the Fish Short Story Prize. Her stories have been Highly Commended in WriteTime competitions and the 2023 King Lear Prizes. She has an MA in Creative Writing from the University of Chichester, and an MA in Literature and the Visual Arts from the University of Reading.

No Further Questions **Kate Twitchin**

Kate retired to live by the sea in Cornwall where she began writing again after a break of about thirty years. She regularly enters short story and flash fiction competitions, enjoying some wins and some listings. Her poems have appeared in *The People's Friend*, writing magazines and online.

August 2 **Ed Walsh**

Ed Walsh is a writer of as yet unpublished novels and occasionally published short stories. He has been writing sporadically since late teenage years when he had some short stories published in small magazines, mainly in America. More recently he has completed three novels, two novellas and several short stories.

The Floodgates   **Moira Warr**

From a young age I've always enjoyed dabbling in writing and have had several stories and articles published in magazines. In 2021, my children's novel called *Trapped in Time With the Bullyraggers* was published by Blossom Spring Publishing. I am currently working on another children's novel. I am a retired teacher.

Trespass   **Mike Watson**

Mike Watson is a prize-winning short story writer and children's author. He has had articles published in fishing, wine, gardening and wildlife magazines. Mike's childhood memoir, *Over the Wall* was broadcast by Radio Newcastle and in 2007 he was commissioned to create fishingexpert.co.uk.

Imagine   **Alun Williams**

I am a Welsh-speaking Welshman from North Wales. I have been writing for about 30 years now, on various websites, mostly Critters-bar.com and have had several stories published in UK and US mags and websites. My favourite genre is crime, especially American and Scandi noir.